"With bold insight and dancing language, Keith Hamilton Cobb delivers this collection of stories that explore the depth and complexities of sex and its aftermath. His concern is not the act, but the residue it leaves upon the heart. The stories, in both length and content, reveal the varied nature of human response to the (sometimes) desperate search for intimacy. He manages, quite meticulously, to traverse the dimensions of sexuality and sexual knowing without entering the realm of the pornographic. His eye is keen. His voice audacious. His structure daring. His words offer a light into the dimensions of the soul's demand for freedom."

Daniel Black, Ph.D.
(Omotosho Jojomani)

Professor of English and African American Studies
Clark Atlanta University/Morehouse College

They Tell Me of a Home
The Sacred Place
Perfect Peace
Twelve Gates to the City

The Odd Purgatory
of My Personal Perception

Little Portraits...

Keith Hamilton Cobb

Heavy Elements Press
New York

Library of Congress Control Number: 2015901894

Editor: Hilary Parry
Cover design: Teddi Black
Original cover art: Keith Hamilton Cobb

Printed in the United States of America

For my Loco Girl

Contents

Author's Note

I don't know if there are really any stories here. No new ones, anyway...

If there are, they're stories of small noises and big silences.

Adepts and gurus everywhere will tell us that there's a lot to be gotten in silence.

But we are inundated in the din that we've created of our time here. And the flesh is "too too solid" in the extreme.

(That's to say, the slappin' around we regularly receive has made us insensitive.)

It's easy to honor our spirits, the loving part of us, when we're not in our bodies. But bodiless, without our animal, a word like "honor" has no meaning.

Nor does "comfort."

Nor does "fear."

There are no words left.

Even "love" has ceased to be a noun...or a verb.

Between the being and the doing there is space. That's where we happen...

...in small noises and big silences.

KHC

They would come, saying,

"Have me. Make me
Blush. Make me
Tremble. Make me
Come to you.
Come for me. With me.
Use me.
Explore. Confuse me. Make me
Laugh. More. Adore me. Make me
Hurt.
Hurt me.
Hold me
Hard. Kiss me with intent.
Exhaust me.
Exalt me. Be
Brave with me.
Elate me.
Embarrass me. Make me
Weep with you. Fall breathless
Into sleep
With you.
It's all good.
It's all love.
I am *love."*

Roland and Maria

Roland's voice had aged more than he had. Grown bassy and tired with twenty years of waiting on the coming days to make good on the promises he'd wishfully assumed they had made, it gave him away to the silence as he sat on the edge of the bed falteringly intoning the words of a Sondheim song, "Maria," to the woman lying asleep, who *had* aged, but in whose peaceful face he could still see the way she looked at him when he was only a whimsical and fleeting concern of hers; the way she looked at him when they were in high school; when nothing longer than a passing glance would conjure a week's worth of fantasy and leave him, at week's end, longing for another if only to reaffirm what he thought he had seen in her eyes when last they had so carelessly taken his measure.

It wasn't a song for a struggling, untrained, almost tenor, but it was her name, living in him with all she hadn't been, and all she was, in him, flowing forth to fill the moments of failing technique so that, on nights with no one to witness, there was always a moment or two, of "Maria," risen above a mumbled ditty and crooned so purely as to still the cicadas in the tree outside the bedroom window.

In the near morning's darkness he would leave buttoning his work shirt, knowing he would never say "I love you" with the lights on.

Inside, upstairs, Maria snored softly in a sound, untroubled sleep. She never looked for love anymore. In the evening, Roland would come back and take his shirt off. He hadn't aged except in his voice, and even that—in the way he said to her, "How are you?"—that hadn't changed at all.

Dahlia

The problem, he found, in the romancing of women considerably younger than he, was the regularly recurring compulsion to scold them. Not the sort of chuckling rebukes that lovers often toss at one another. But spasmodic paroxysms of vitriol, urging some young paramour to act her age, aborted in the throat and choked back in pain upon his simultaneous realization that she was, in fact. Choked back before she had heard, before she had caught the slight scent of disdain, and, with it then forever in the air, begun to consider that he might not, in all good faith, be her willing accomplice in joy. And if she were to find him out, she would simply find another who would be. Because she was young and beautiful, and, given the vast, intemperate palette of her sexual prospects and notions that made her wet, she was easily indifferent. And he was afraid.

The case of Dahlia was no exception. She was twenty-four, and the experience of her body, naked and wanting, in among him and his sheets, her skin after climax nearly recalescent on a cool afternoon, might just as well have been heroin. It was sexual certainly, but not sex simply, or lust, or fucking of any sort per se. Rather, for him, it was something more in kind with addiction, a dependency developed inadvertently, but in the end entirely, for a particular piece of moving, interactive art. He could devour the view from down on her across the rippled contours of her stomach contracting and relaxing in waves as she came as often as he cared to facilitate for the best part of one hour into the next. Then lie back and watch her, breasts heaving as she lay there in a sheen of sweat owning his bed, panting out the remainder of any hour left unutilized into an overtaking stillness; into an almost sleep from which his slightest touch would arouse her once again, and they would play on, she riding spread and trembling on the living altar of his undivided attention, he, chasing her abandon like a mendicant, hoping perhaps to catch the crumbs of her blissful unconcern. True Elysium or contrived opiate, the sensual symbiosis of theirs, perpetual but uneven, was got him for the forfeiture of anything akin to an engaging comment or conversation. What's more, it was had at the expense of several lies he would tell himself, the most egregious of which might very well have been that, beyond the bounds of that sex-smell bed, she could fully, or even remotely appreciate anything else he was or aspired to. For Dahlia, when not enraptured in the throes of orgasm, had notions of her own, and dreams, and a sense of self completely appropriate to any twenty-four-year-old's frame of reference. Ensconced in the magic mantle of her youth, she remained alluringly inane and blameless. He, on the other hand, having long since outgrown the once impenetrable cloak of his boyhood, returned mourning it, returned, ashamedly, like a junkie, and returned again, to make love to her jealously; passionately but resentful, and forever angry, at himself.

Mickey Montgomery
and the Gelson's Girl

E rrands on a Tuesday… Just a few easy things, like the clean-
ers and the bank, but that very stuff that eats up a day no
matter how you plan it on the driving-essential/parking-if-pos-
sible island of L.A., and Mickey rolled up at a quarter to four to
the Gelson's Market in West Hollywood; into that lull after the
lunch rush, and before the pick-something-up-for-dinner-just-
off-work crowd began to swarm the joint. His sweat-dampened
denim shirt stuck to him in spots. That would happen to those
who drove around in open-topped cars, and were not so particular
about moving quickly from one climate-controlled environment
to the next. They looked wind-blown and tousled, with color in
their skin, and dusted with a humanizing layer of road dirt. They
looked imperfect, like people. His tattered and paint-dirty jeans
rode low for the way sweat made them loose in the waist, and
he looked younger, more like an aging surfer boy than he could
claim credit for. He wasn't younger, he was just unplanned, with
a betraying day or two old crop of salt-and-pepper stubble on
his face. And he was lean, and his face and arms and sandaled
feet were browned by the sun. Except for his military cut—his
gray hair was short, and flat on top like a marine—it all looked
devoid of intelligent design; the eclectic culmination of circumstance and an artist's focus being perpetually occupied elsewhere.
And his haphazard handsomeness tended to turn the heads of

many of the eligibles in the heart of Boy's Town. In his passing interactions there on the neighborhood streets, in the shops and places to eat, he could not but note that he could say or not say, do or not do, and it *all* ended up meaning something comprehensive to the gay men who seemed to find him, through no conscious efforts of his own, a thing to be desired. He had become a common occurrence on his several walking trajectories throughout town, or pulling his filthy old blue Bronco into a parking space on Santa Monica Boulevard blasting Italian opera and talking aloud to the wolfhound, Padraig, panting in repose on the back seat. And he had grown used to being seen. Who didn't take some validation from being seen, really? It was Los Angeles after all. Some spoke, some propositioned, some just stared. And one could do worse, he would often remind himself, than to be looked at with longing by anyone. And maybe, he would need to concede with a private smile, the aesthetic he assumed was not so completely inadvertent after all.

Twice in two days chance had it that he'd found himself there in the market, in the "Twelve Items or Less" line specifically, breezing through in what, to his memory, had always been an intolerably busy store.

"Two days in a row," noted aloud from across the counter the bookish little Asian derived cashier with the long, obsidian black ponytail of thick, straight hair, remembering him as she watched through black, horn-rimmed glasses his two cans of non-stick cooking spray and two six-packs of Corona roll up to her on the conveyor belt. "Yesterday, about this same time... Just the beer though," she said, tilting her head back to look, just so briefly, up and into his face who stood a true foot and a half above her, and then back to the task at hand.

"Yeah," he said smiling as he recalled her, and her ponytail, how her hair was dense, really like the tail of a pony, and how the big glasses on her face against her ethnic features, magnifying her big, almond eyes, were reminiscent of a derogatory World War II cartoon. "Well, now I know when to come," he said, tapping on the face of his watch for emphasis.

"That's good," she said, without smiling, taking another quick perusal of him over the tops of her heavy frames, and yet, perhaps not quite deliberate. "Most guys generally *don't* know when to come."

The bagger, an acutely disinterested youth with a vast array of extraneous metal pieces impaling the flesh of his face and more sundry data indelibly etched upon his skin than he could have possibly lived enough life to articulate reasons for, inquired about paper or plastic in little more than a mumble. Mickey didn't hear him. He was otherwise engaged in looking hard askance at the checker—who now ignored his attention as she went about ringing up his goods—thinking she appeared far too newly post-adolescent to have wit deep or sexuality developed enough to deftly throw a joke like that across the counter at one such as he. He was otherwise engaged in attempting to resolve that it hadn't been a joke at all he'd just heard out of her, but only a simple statement of fact about the shopping patterns of the customers of Gelson's; a comment regarding the clock-work precision with which they lined up at the counter from four-fifteen to five-thirty; a comment suggesting that those she judged smart would find their way to the market before or after the rush… Of course it was. Banter at the check-out, behind them now, and meaningless as she tended to the register with a focused nonchalance offering no acknowledgement that they had shared a charged moment. They hadn't... Had they?

She was the smallest of things, with delicate hands, and equally fragile features made funny by her thick-rimmed glasses, a style choice that Mickey found somehow working regardless. When she caught eyes with him again it was to announce his total. "Twenty-four dollars and sixty-eight cents," she said in a clear, pleasant voice with no hint of an accent, too full and resonant to have risen from her little frame, and teasing at experiences beyond her years. And then, nothing, but an enigmatic stare through thick lenses, expectant of remittance, and perhaps something else that Mickey, disconcerted, was too couth to speak to, but plenty lewd-minded enough to stand dumbly reflecting upon. Was it all only the noxious effluvium of his disreputable imagination? Had there been, seated on some shelf high upon the rear wall of his brain, some unobtrusive schoolgirl fantasy that he hadn't ever given healthy attention to, now rattling about loudly in his not-so-full cranial cavity, having been knocked loose by just such an implausible instance and caricature as this, animated by an offhand remark ripe to be read into? She had little else to recommend her. Leastwise nothing that he could see, covered as it all was by the unflattering brown grocery worker togs. She was skinny, and small-breasted, hipless, and Asian-assed, though, if one left Boy's Town, one could find an entire section in the Porn Emporium dedicated to the barely legal variety of waif that looked just like her, catching all kinds of flesh and liking it from guys five times her size. And Mickey found himself suddenly moved to concede that, apparently, a somewhat smaller but no less triple-X-rated section of the same had long been stuffed just behind the door of his own fertile fancy, now kicked open by a benign exchange with a child young enough by far to be his daughter. And there the magazines and videos lay, tumbled out of his closet of dreams, and strewn upon the conveyor belt that ran between them with a dull hum. He pretended not to notice as he, flustered, fished from his pocket the twenty-five bucks, fumbling about with the bills, uncrumpling them enough to discern a twenty and some singles, dropping loose coins onto the floor, then handing what he held across the counter to her cupped in his upturned palms as he looked up to discover her again eyeing him, still and expectant, over horn-rimmed glasses. She took the cash from his hands and turned toward the register again while the eyes lingered, almost, lagging for a swollen, suggestive second, maybe, behind her body as it shifted away, leaving after them the probability of her innocence confusingly, uncomfortably, arousingly diluted by the whetted possibility that it didn't exist.

The bagger, lacking a response to the question that defined his job entire, oblivious in equal measure to cashier and patron alike, had done the only thing that thoughtlessness could have (and what the inanity of American merchandising had taught him). He posited Mickey's items in both paper *and* plastic. Mickey didn't much notice for being too busy struggling to dismiss all that his prurient imaginings had surely larded onto the non-event of this community college girl simply trying to pay her tuition and being, at instances, congenial. He was feeling nearly confident enough that he had, within the brief space of their interaction, assessed the potentialities, guiltily indulged them in satisfactory detail, and, with a self-surprising reluctance, gathered up all the lurid media from where it had spilled onto the conveyor belt and stuffed it all back into the pantry of his subconscious. Wrestling to get the cabinet door closed, he lifted the grocery bag from the counter top and held out his hand once more to receive his change. The checker dropped a quarter, a nickel, and two pennies into his open palm counting in that same chest-resonant voice, "Twenty-five, thirty, one, thirty-two cents…" It was the cognitive dissonance caused him by the weight of her voice in conflict with her diminutive stature, but also the way that she sounded as though she might have been counting out change to a 2nd grader that disquieted him, that and the way she then immediately turned her attention to the woman standing behind him in line whose goods were now moving forward on the belt.

Distractedly, oddly dejected, he turned, pocketing the coins and stooping to collect the few others that had just previously found their way to the floor. Then he'd taken the first six or so steps away from the counter and towards the exit.

Through the crack in the door of the closet of dreams that, in all the confusion, he had never quite managed to slam shut and lock, he saw himself kissing her goodbye; kissing her upturned face where she knelt there at his feet, naked but for her heavy black glasses which intensified her deep, brown eyes gazing imploringly up at him, still wet with tears of adoration, begging him to stay, her lips parted and still wet with—when he heard her voice from behind him say, in those deep, grounded tones that only honesty and awareness made, "Most guys generally don't know *where* to come either…" When he turned to look she was already on to ringing up the dozen or so items of the next patron. Without looking up she said, "Cool jeans…" But the patron was wearing a skirt.

Leo

Leo Louisi looked into the mirror and he saw his age. His face was flaccid and sunken some below the cheekbones. His skin was rough and dry. He had smoked it to how it was, and he had drunk it to how it was, and now there was little to do to pretty it up but smooth his moustache and arrange his hair. He did that often, autonomically.

One of the last couple of rent boys he'd bedded both at once had given him something that embarrassed him. It was not so much in the having that he was embarrassed, "Ya lay down wit dogs and whannot…" but in the degrading, clinical process of the ridding himself of it, to do with topicals that could perhaps be applied with dignity, but with never the first pretense of grace at all. After all, he could see himself in the bathroom mirror where, like everywhere else, it was his tendency to carry himself for the most part with, albeit a weariness, a refinement as well. Or a stilted finesse that attracted him still to life when he found it reflected there… He checked regularly on that reflection to make *sure* it was still there, and, if it were not, to make sure he made whatever adjustment in demeanor and carriage he needed in order to restore it. His long, cranky body cracked and popped in the joints when he moved with a labored elegance; the peaceful comportment of a self-assured but always just slightly drunken tribal elder of an extinct tribe…dutifully applying an assortment of ointments to his anus…and having to laugh.

Having sworn off whores, he had been too long in solitude. "Touch deprived" would probably be a better way than most to have described it. Too long absent the laying on of hands, or lips, or other anatomy through which an inarticulate and otherwise unreleasable energy can flow; too inactive a too integral element of his life force quickened only in the giving, even if it was that he had, at times, to buy those to whom he gave it. If not vital, that contact of the flesh, then simply longed for with an intensity that grew in proportion to the time he spent alone. And he was most often alone, because he drove people from him when he drank, not as a mean, obnoxious drunk will, but as a smelly one, reeking of alcohol and stale cigarette smoke and coffee, those ingredients through him and out again at pores commingling in a body odor that all who knew him recognized as uniquely his. Chief among ironies was that, except for that, he was loved, deeply and dearly. There was shelter sought and respite taken beneath the praiseful gaze of those eyes he had of opalescent gray-brown. His smiling mouth of worn, browning teeth; a full, sensual, southern-Italian mouth, spoke kindnesses in a hoarse and tattered Brooklynese, and loving assurances to everyone, no different from the days on the stoop, when his teeth were still straight and white, with Danny Drake and O'Toole.

"The sweetest kid in the neighborhood you got," said the Drake boy's mother to Rita Louisi, when she would worry about him out loud as they sat at the tea table placed in the window above, and Leo's voice from down in the street bounced off the building walls how 'Toole was sure to win the 11th grade creative writing competition because he was "wonaful, his writin' and whannot. Just so byoodiful…"

"A little too sweet, maybe, God forbid," she'd whisper back sometimes beneath her breath, as if it were a secret.

And Nettie Drake would pat her hand and say, "You don't worry. God loves him, that's all that matters. And you see if God doesn't look after him." And then they'd look down where Danny and the O'Toole kid slouched and sprawled on the steps, and Leo, with the big, jet black Saturday Night Fever hair, in blaring skin-tight Qiana, stood over them laughing and talking at them at the top of his voice.

"Dat one you wrote, about the army…'The Parade' uh thing? 'The Parade uh…Ground,' yeah? Dat was so poetical. Just byoodiful. Cuz' I remember I was like, 'hand t' God, dis beats d' fuckin' shit outta Ethan Frome fa' real.' They should put your shit in d' textbook. Right, Danny, right?"

"Leo, you watch your mouth!" Mrs. Louisi would holler down from the second floor. "You don't say God's name wit dat filthy mouth!"

Danny nodded his agreement and smiled up at him, entranced by his beneficent fire. 'Toole, who never could accept a compliment as easily as he would spark and flame to an insult, slouched there allaying Leo's lavish praise by demurring with macho indifference. Leo, a gentle, giant, eternal god of mirth, stood like a laughing prophet holding forth to his disciples, but stood really only for not wanting to soil his perfect, pressed white double-knits on the street-dirty stoop.

It made him do strange things. The pent up reservoir of emotion came out at his eyes, and in the expressions of an intense goodness that resided in his face and carriage. But mostly, the only mechanism to vent it fully was so ill-designed as to offer it egress only in another's embrace. Expression was easier back when, and release. Unthought-on in youth, there was no self-editing the forms of joy. Now, this sensual congestion, it made him regard his weathered middle age too long in mirrors. He started with that in the early nineties, when Danny got AIDS and died. Nettie Drake, grieving, marveled how no one ever knew that he had a needle drug problem. He didn't, but she still marveled, and Leo, and all the mothers, were content to let her. But from then, he began to note with a passing trepidation the pace of his own evolving visage, which had clearly begun a steady, solemn forced march towards something that no one with his or Danny's aesthetic sense could call attractive. Sometimes he would catch himself peering, brow furrowed, at the storefront glass. Looking deep into the reflection for any of life's beautiful reasons that were no longer always just there, but now often hid camouflaged in creases of skin and the cloud cover of eyes, he would unfurrow, and begin combing over his thinning patch with his cracked and yellowed fingers, forgetting that they held a cigarette. Then, awakened, he would move off giggling at his own self-conceit, rather loving Leo a little bit again, even as he ruined the delicate hair repair by brushing the ashes out of it.

Elvin, the O'Toole kid, who won the 11th grade creative writing competition, was a first lieutenant in the army who might have retired the year he took it in Desert Storm. All the mothers that were left were pretty shaken up by that. Leo was too, and grieved silently, but fiercely, that 'Toole had had to face death so far from home in the employ of a "Don't ask, Don't tell" army that was so unlike the one he had written about with such raw, untaught eloquence and admiration in his short story, "The Parade Ground." That story, their English teacher had tightly allowed as "good, but inappropriate." The competition judges had called it "extraordinary," and "excellent," and Danny Drake had said with a commiserative sadness that only Leo, and perhaps Elvin recognized, "It's so fuckin' good, but, uh, whadya call that word, uhm, unplausible…I think." Elvin's father never read it, and was proud Elvin had served, and died, like a man.

But the months of mourning went by and Leo would still lead with that smile and those eyes, and that language of embrace and uplift that he had for even the dumpster diggers out behind his building. He would cheer everybody when he came out to the boroughs visiting the mothers from over on the Upper West where he still had the place that he'd bought with the one partner who'd stayed the longest and then died of one of those sorts of things that older men would.

"Prostate Cancer?!" Leo recalled nothing more vividly about the day he received the news of his partner's stage four diagnosis than wanting to ask Danny, "Who has dat shit? Fuckin' old dudes, right, Danny, right?" But Danny had died.

And so now, there were the other days—depending upon how long ago last some paid paramour had given him, by the abandon of his movements and the urgency of his breath, to believe that he was truly blessed to be the focus of Leo's amorous attentions—the mirror lined elevator in his building would ride up and down for half an hour or more, passengers embarking and disembarking with hardly a notice, they having long since become accustomed to Leo standing in one corner of the car staring silently at his reflection, at times adjusting his posture, repairing his hair, or amending the expression on his face.

Katherine Tells Her Next Ex-Lover a Thing or Two

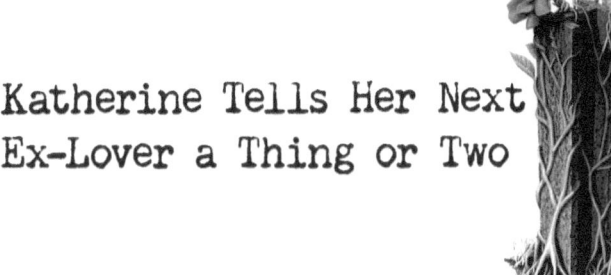

K atherine liked Black men. She was drawn to them sexually, by no means exclusively among men, but *certainly* among them. The age-worn clichés could hold true from case to case or not. Energetically, there *was* a difference. She felt it in different ways, and at different places on her skin than anything that "the white fellas" induced. Like the last thing that Reuben, the bar man, had said to her through large, brown lips that might have been sculpted out of some soft stone. "Nah. Y'ain't payin', Sully. You can tip the bar back or whateva, but he gone home. I don't want none a' your money." A simple sentence or two, clipped and slanged to tax the muscles of the mouth little if at all. But in his quiet nonchalance of speech and carriage, Katherine felt a presence that few white boys appeared to possess, at least anymore. A latent force that bided its time, perhaps in reserve, she would muse, for the addressing of matters that hundreds of years of far more pressing burdens had labeled "Of Issue" in the African American male DNA. Whatever the case, she was taken to just watching him amble about behind the bar. She appreciated Reuben involuntarily—inexplicably arousing energies notwithstanding—for being just the sort of man that her Irish father would have hated, he having hated reflexively all Black men for his awareness of those same sensual energies of theirs—and for fear it was just the sort of thing that his daughter might too enthusiastically appreciate. It was inevitable. Reuben's forearms flexed as he lifted a case of beer from the floor onto the back bartop. He winked at her as he turned to see her watching him, then bent at the waist to pick up another one. She winked back as he rose again. She smiled, tickled nearly to laughter at his still, expressionless attention; the laminate surfacing a sexuality imaginably in such vast reserve, she mused, that it bloody well should'a frightened the fuck out a' her old man. She was slightly drunk, but giddy mostly with the irony.

"Sully" was how she was called, from girlhood, and now, in her transient social circles. She was a big-boned Irish woman of business from the City of New York. All crimson hair, and a whiskey voice, and the life-weary resignation in her eyes of her potato farmer ancestors. And she had come to Los Angeles to find that there was an ownership missing from it. She had come to find that it had been populated by people who seemed to know no ownership of themselves.

An MBA with no personal stake in The Dream Machine, she had volunteered for a winter stint in the LA office. Manhattan was bitter cold and she'd come for the warmth, and to be able to say she had seen it; to be able to tell her underwriter associates back on the block that she had been unimpressed. They had always suggested she'd love it, and she had always expressed doubt. Now she could unequivocally affirm what her ancillary association to the movie business had always made her suspect. No one took responsibility for Hollywood, what it was or wasn't, so far as she was able to ascertain. No one took responsibility for contriving the rationale upon which it was built, elaborately woven to legitimize business detached from humanity, beauty, or truth.

Such detachment, by and large, is the definition of business, and certainly something to which any business school graduate worthy of their diploma could attest. Nothing new in itself, except that, to her, the brash and raucous glare of "The Industry" seemed perpetually to be struggling too hard to hide its self-loathing beneath a threadbare tapestry, elaborately woven as it was, of self-aggrandizement. It was, Katherine observed, forever convening galas and red carpet convocations to confer upon itself awards for the very humanity, beauty, and truth that were so inconvenient to its own existence. Russell Crowe, she thought, exhibited an admirable self-ownership.

Beyond him, however, and his ephemeral attraction, she tended to look straight through the diaphanous front of airs and attitudes. It was her refusal to suffer the grandiosity of fools at all—a genetic inheritance—that made her intimidating to many in the left neck of the woods. Though a fascination with the science of money—perhaps another genetic inheritance—had lifted her up out of the old neighborhood and compelled her through graduate school, she could still muster no empathy for this culture of highly wrought rationale justifying the depth of mendacity under the moniker of business.

Nor could she quietly abide the lie that Hollywood was something other than a sprawling, smog-shrouded suburb. It was not an actual city at all. It did not sing, or make any signature sounds as Manhattan did, or even Chicago. Its only apology for its artificial existence (Where did the water come from to grow all that grass on the chaparral?) was in the lemming-like lives of its inhabitants, who would walk about shamefaced if they tended even a little towards introspection. But that too was inconvenient. Instead, they made little eye contact in the best case, since with eye contact comes accountability, as any big-boned Irish woman of business from the City of New York will tell you. It was a culture of liars; of people who lied, to themselves and to one another, and not to be respected, her father might have said, but to be taken advantage of surely; to be used for the sole purpose of "puttin' quarters in your own kick." That's how they used each other. And they were not alone. The latter-day world of business, perhaps the latter-day world, was this dynamic throughout it. People were this way. But Hollywood was where she was.

Offered straight up and unsolicited to anyone who might care to listen, many found Katherine's perspective, if intimidating, also irresistibly attractive as part in parcel of her physical package. Her entire aesthetic, so un-Hollywood, was wrapped in a brazen willingness to commit to an innate sensibility irrespective of whom it might impress or offend. Sully looked at things and saw what she saw through the discerning eyes of her New York Irish, old neighborhood ethos that offered no rationale intricately spun up to support it. The people from which she'd sprung, for better or worse, stood in their own trumped-up truths on strong peasant legs and challenged all comers to step up and do something about it. But also, like the Jews, and the Italians, and the Blacks, their cultural inadequacies, of which each was well aware, as well as their enduring strengths, were the seat of the sort of folkloric forthrightness that made people tend to tacitly agree, even when they found themselves to be the object of its critical focus.

Her father's racism was as innate a sensibility, and as unapologetically committed to as any of her own. She had to respect him, even though his unwillingness to evolve his perspective heightened the irony that she giggled at, and, while he lived, expanded the distance from him from which she did her giggling… Perhaps Hollywood, if it could find a cumulative voice, would laugh at her when she returned home. It would have every right to. But, she suspected, it would amble on oblivious, and emptily uncommitted.

Katherine took full responsibility for all that she was, and cared little about what she wasn't, courting the advent of middle-age with Bushmills and cigarettes while holding it at bay with a treadmill regimen that she said, "the like a' would'a put an Olympic athlete in a coma." Her age and how it accentuated her ethnicity shown in her face. Nicotine and the Los Angeles sun were not friends to her fair Irish skin. Deepening crow's feet and laugh lines suggested a feminine character not often spotted in the LA nightlife, eschewing artificial "enhancement" in favor of the darkening freckles that dotted and framed her Celtic nose, fanning out onto the less than silky smooth skin of a farm girl's cheeks. This too was magnetic, her un-posed, unassuming beingness in a town where perfection is perpetually sought regardless of that same town's inability to define it. Of course, there was the enticement of the body-tight dresses in which she sheathed her pin-up poster girl figure; the days-long, muscled legs accentuated by the severe Rodeo Drive pumps that she had had fun shopping for. But many women, particularly of the Hollywood variety, had achieved that requisite aspect when the occasion called for it. Regardless of all, from clothing to the rigors of her daily routine, Katherine was alluringly at home in her own aging skin, and that made all the difference.

Manhattanites, if they've lived there long enough to call

themselves natives, have a way of recognizing one another even if they have never met. Or perhaps in the old country… Maybe there were ghosts of Donegal in him seven or eight generations old and restless for communion with something familiar. Then maybe he was drawn to her for the same reason that most all were. Katherine's was a pronounced and contradictory presence, standing at the bar of any one of her downtown haunts. Downtown, where she was drawn, where, if people wouldn't talk, she could almost pretend she was back in New York. Where the men down from Hollywood with their dates, lured by the gentrified resurgence of new clubs and nightlife, would step over their significant others in order to get next to her for even a moment under the pretense of one ridiculous platonic overture or another; to light her next smoke where it hung as if by some sensual magic from her thick lower lip as her deep brown eyes began to cast about in search of a match; or to buy her the next whiskey no sooner than her glass had once again made contact with the bar after she'd tossed it back in a flying pyrotechnical display of long, lush, fiery red hair. "Irish chicks," she would offer in her sleepy rasp of a voice with a hard dying New York brogue that seemed to make her self-deprecation all the more ingenuous, "those old country, broad-hipped, baby-makin', steel cut oatmeal Irish babes, with their round faces and little upturned noses, can look like piglets. But if you got lips, and a lot of us don't, we can look like very sexy ones. If I do say so my damned self."

And then, the gent from New York was somewhat of a contradiction himself, at least at first. He was handsomely built. Broad shouldered and tall, he was nothing hard on the eyes, and a little too well-dressed. He wore his shirt collar buttoned-up, and not even the knot of his tie askew, some minor dishevelment being practically a prerequisite for anyone who would be found still wearing a suit in a bar at 2 A.M. He overheard Katherine holding forth to the bartender on the myriad merits of strong Irish women, and while she was not beautiful, strictly speaking (for she said as much), or young, as in general were the women that tended to make themselves available to the potentialities suggested by his high-dollar demeanor, he thought perhaps he might have known her. Or, what is attraction? Her rough grace was arousing. Her candor exposed a character that he and others recognized as authentic, and wished it were theirs.

But the guy from New York was really a guy from Peabody, Massachusetts, and the closest he could honestly claim to a big city pedigree was four years at Boston College. He had done his business school homework and made of himself a minor celebrity on Wall Street, with a Tribeca property, a little young gun prestige, and a healthy sense of invincibility, all by the deeply insightful age of thirty. Much of this Katherine, between her own education and the inherited insights of her elders, would be able to surmise. But it was superfluous. It was all the data of person that she'd have neither time nor interest enough to consider as anything but extraneous as he passed through her sphere, she guarding the entrance, and more than ready to show him the exit when all of immediate worth had been ascertained.

For now, she clocked his approach as she continued her banter with the barman. This was another thing she had learned from her father. To stay aware, "like a horse," of what was advancing from any angle, not however like a horse to run, but to be prepared to check it in its tracks if it were anything undesired. A look could do that. The Sullivans bore a countenance that did not so much threaten as disquiet with the focus of armed, attentive disregard. She knew, even from a distance, that he was no native of the Island—either of them.

What she saw walking with admirable authority towards her along the bar when she finally took a headlong glance was a sturdy, good-looking kid, showing up just on the interesting side of that well-styled, hard-bodied metrosexual sensibility, which time and money will buy in less and less attractive overabundance if one isn't careful. Neither native New Yorkers, nor old neighborhood Irishmen tended to bother with that sort of department store peacock shit. That was for the Europeans and the Middle Easterners who had bought up seven-eighths of the city, and for the Wall Street boys expecting their numbers to turn them into men, who were still just too young to "know any fuckin' better."

What *he* saw—what everyone saw—was a woman who wore the countenance, and commanded the equipment of one who had seen a goodly piece of life, was wise, and without pretense. What he saw was one who could execute her trivial or deepest desires without ambivalence or embarrassment, and could easily offer a fellow the experience of being expertly fucked into catatonia when and as she chose. And this was something that the young ones, for all their soft skin and sweet smells, were not nearly so accomplished at. What they *did* have was shorter stories. And for that alone men had historically sacrificed prowess. Katherine, however, with her muscle tone, aging elegance, and self-serving insouciance offered something perhaps built of the best of both worlds. And it was all of this for which he braved the unnerving intensity of her casual regard, taking the stool beside her as the bartender was pouring the next round and tossing his Amex Platinum card onto the bar with no great ostentation, but with a practiced care to be conspicuous.

"Let me," he said. Then, a bit too dismissively to the barman who tiredly eyed his card and then him with an aged knowledge of not person but type, "Run us a tab, Coach. Have you got Midleton?" Then, "Very Rare," he added for whose benefit no one knew.

"It ain't tuna, Seamus, it's whiskey," Katherine said in her throaty giggle, making Reuben laugh out loud despite his usually unflappable decorum. From where she sat, points off for pretentiousness did not necessarily lessen the boy's bedmate potential. She was, in the end, a realist, and forgiving despite her wicked streak. The romance lives of wanderers and business travelers were most often a perpetual making due in the moment, provided, of course, that too many red flags weren't waving prior to closing time.

"Nah, I got Jameson," Reuben said, "Same company," setting a glass before the man-child in the $240.00 tie who wrinkled his nose disapprovingly like a little boy disdaining Brussels sprouts.

"Bushmills then, just like my compatriot," he responded as he took the full measure of Katherine's face, and she looked back, amused by the monetarily supported moxie of this clean-shaven mooncalf, with the nice lips, and a map of The Republic imprinted upon his forehead. "Those are some eyes," he said, holding her gaze. Then, filling the space absent a response, he extended his hand and offered, "Evan," with a broad, pristine grin that must have wowed 'em back in the Manhattan haunts of the artificially wealthy white kids.

Her eyes having long been admired, in honesty or not, to the point of cliché, wandered languidly, and somewhat disinterestedly away and went looking for a cigarette. The good stewards of California had recently decided that smoking in public establishments should not be legal. And much of the rest of the country, because, as Katherine said, "They're followers," were following. But it only made closing time that much more attractive in several ways to the scarlet scofflaw. After hours, if she'd forged a friendship like Reuben's, once doors were locked, and if lights were again brought low, as sometimes they'd be in deference to her endearing presence, she could recreate that haze that endemically hovered in barrooms when she was a girl, and she could look out from within it, and from beneath her brow surveying for the 2 A.M. hanger-on who wasn't ugly, or stupid drunk. This night, as most, the selection was slim. The two young women remaining, who had sat together nursing their last call cocktails into the ugly lights and into the Katherine-deferential darkness again, got up to leave, apparently concluding that Johnny Armani had made *his* choice. The place was empty.

"Pour you one too," was Katherine's placid dictate to Reuben, who held out a lighter in one hand while retrieving a third glass with the other.

Katherine caressed and steadied the hand holding the lighter that Reuben held forth to her, gently with strong fingers, as she held her hair back from the flame. Her newly manicured and painted nails belied a pair of hands that might no less efficiently, fisted, displace a jaw as embrace it in contemplation of kissing.

Glancing back, the boy, having not yet abandoned the expectation of a handshake, held *his* hand suspended in space and attentively waited. So, dragging deeply, her addiction playing like high-end porn, her cigarette reposing between parted and liquor-wetted lips, Katherine, through the miasma that rose up to caress her face, in a languid exhalation, like the final suspiration of a dying dragon, looked at him, considered, and at length spoke.

"So…what brings *you* to Tinseltown, Paddy?"

"Evan," he corrected, and waited. And so she raised an eyebrow, and waited.

And so he continued, "I'm partner in a consortium that's got a piece of an Adam Sandler picture. They flew me out here to see what's what."

Her raised, red eyebrow, betraying her less than total indifference, Evan took as encouragement, and said, "And how 'bout you?…"

"I work for the guys that probably floated your completion bond. Adam Sandler, huh?… I guess there's no accountin' for taste."

"Who gives a shit? Accounting is for money." Aptly spoken facts always made Sully smile.

"This to that," she shined, raising her glass and dumping its contents down her long, open throat without a swallow. Such sensual spectacles as these had left many a man dumbstruck with a hard-on in the past. But Evan reached for his glass and held it up, appearing relieved rather to have found something at last to do with his outstretched hand.

"And here's to your daddy's daughter," he offered, knocking back a shot, then once more flashing perhaps the whitest teeth that new money could buy.

Worrisome if that were the only tool in his kit, Katherine thought as she drew long and slow on her cigarette and fell once again to a mute appraisal of his face.

Exhaling… Her eyes searching, assessing what there was about the smiling swain that could work. What might she not feel deprived of in the least were she to wander home and see to herself? She had been an endless, uninspiring month already among the actors and sundry other hothouse orchids. Evan had no idea as to how his generally East Coast energies, all less tasteful things else notwithstanding, were tending to work in his favor.

The daughter of Hell's Kitchen, and of Piran Sullivan, a dead Westy chieftain they called "Little Pete," Katherine knew a few things. She knew there wasn't any Hell's Kitchen anymore. In fact, there was hardly a New York as she remembered it from her adolescence, which was all the more reason to love the Manhattan within her. Home for Katherine, for better or worse, was wherever Katherine was.

"You see something interesting?" the boy attempted again with another flash of bright, perfect teeth, perhaps a gambit known to have jump-started many a barroom dalliance in the past, but now playing more like a measure of impatience with Katherine's silent, unbroken perusal. To have answered "yes" would have been as much of a half-truth as to have answered "no." Katherine didn't lie. So she just watched him, contemplating with a suppressed glee his slowly deteriorating deportment in the unanticipated presence of a woman who wasn't impressed enough to flirt, yet, like a horse, a heavy-haunched mare in a field of stupid stallions, alerted. And attentive.

But Googy Quinn worked construction with his father. And one day he fell a full story and a half off a scaffold, landing face first on the concrete that comprised the corner of 46th Street and 11th Avenue. He got up, spit out three teeth, and bled a puddling trail straight to Sullivan's Bar, Pete's place, where the old man made him go to the emergency room and take a dozen stitches in both his upper and lower lip before he'd give him three fingers of the preferred first aid of an Irish laborer. He and Katherine were all of seventeen. And she could remember helping her father wrestle her as angry as he was blood-besmeared beau into the cab and riding with him up to Roosevelt Hospital on 10th at 58th Street. Actually, *she* wrestled, with Pete lending a steadying hand at the end of a stiff arm from time to time, he having long since risen above the status of one who would be expected to soil his clothes with such shenanigans.

Googy had been no Adonis to start, and thereafter always looked somewhat the worse for wear, particularly with that permanent gap in his grin, a purely utilitarian grill for a proletarian man. Still, he was Pete's boy, or the closest he had to one. And as he aged, his relationship to Katherine's dad via Katherine, and even after she'd found more exotic interests to pursue, would render a winning smile as it relates to getting on in the world less and less necessary. At least in the world of the dying neighborhood, and perhaps a few blocks uptown, downtown, and between the rivers, which was the only world that Googy ever knew. He was Pete's boy.

And it wasn't the money itself that stifled the cabbie's grumbling broken English-Russian protestations about Googy's face hemorrhaging all over his back seat. Beside the unstudied, nearly autonomic way Pete Sullivan peeled off two ten-dollar notes for a ride that wouldn't cost four bucks and handed them through the driver-side window, it was the look he leveled. Pete's look. A gentle, lasered lowering out from beneath his eyelids that conveyed an unsettling combination of consideration and menace cowed even the grunting case-hardened Soviet mid-sentence. Also it was how it seemed he barely deigned to shift at the shoulders slightly, slowly panning his gaze to glance through the window into the back seat and catch eyes with his daughter as he refolded his roll of bills and slid it smoothly back into his pants pocket with one fluid motion. One shoulder really—the left one dipped down with a shift of the neck and the slightest bending backward from the waist—elegant and deliberate, instead of a stooping forward as any peasant would have. How he looked back at the cabbie then, and into his eyes as to reaffirm an understanding never spoken. Then how he straightened all of his five foot six, satisfied, and walked away, simply, soundlessly, hands in his pockets, done. As if the first doubt about his specific wishes being carried out, in a life where men will do anything for the right amount of money, was inconceivable. Piran (Little Pete) Sullivan's deep, hard, laughless eyes set a price on everything. It was never the price of the thing itself, but the price of complicity without discussion. Then he came, literally, from the pocket and paid the price he'd set, that look of his searching the faces of all life's petit vendors, from cabbies to cops to borough presidents, for the assurance that no discussion would ever need to be had. It never was.

And Pete was dead now. It would be about six o'clock of a Friday morning in New York. Googy would need to be on the job soon; some job, if he hadn't hit the lottery or found some grift that wasn't some other latter-day Kitchen cabal's personal property. Despite her father's tutelage and protection, he was always more terrier than gangster. He was a proud and pedigreed working dog. And if he was alive and unfettered he was probably just getting to sleep, hoping to jam eight hours into two after drinking into the night. Buying round after round for his crew into the wee hours, he would tear off one hard-earned Jackson after another, not with his mentor's natural grace and manicured hands, but with his own big-hearted vulgarity—making up with largess for what he lacked in Pete Sullivan-style panache—with laughter, gap-toothed, full-throated, warrior-lunged laughter, like a man did; like the generous rough-hewn monarch he was. Then squandering the fleeting early A.M. fucking that poor little, pretty Dominican girlfriend of his damn near to death. He was good for that too. Like that night, returned from the emergency room, in the upper back office of Sullivan's Bar, after his hero's welcome home, Katherine gone all Florence Nightingale with concern and Marilyn Chambers with adoration, bare-assed on the disrupted and scattered desktop, her panties torn free and hanging from one thigh, legs flung wide and wrapped around his draft horse haunches while Googy, whose given name was Gobban, after some Celtic god of blacksmiths, hammered away with near half a bottle of Jameson in him, and a fist full of Vicodin into the bargain.

To Googy she lifted a glass and slammed it back, slapped it to the bartop, and shuddered through the face and neck, sucking in the savor of whiskey through her teeth. Then she took another look at Mickey-of-the-silver-spoon sitting opposite her and wondered, really, if this were allowed to continue, if he could possibly measure up. For the present, Evan held his own. As if determined to establish a momentum that Katherine, in her revels, was just as determined to break, "Give us two more," he barked, tapping his empty glass on the bartop impatiently and beckoning to the barman who had begun to shut down his bar. Reuben, strolling over particularly slowly in answer to all of Evan's presumed authority, carried the bottle of Bushmills at his side, holding the neck of it in an overhand fist as if he might at any moment lift it up and hit the boy across the head with it. He poured two more. Evan again shoved his Platinum card, which was still lying there without the least acknowledgment of any sort having yet been made to it, across the bar. It's said that the definition of insanity is the repeating of the same action while expecting a different result. But we work with the tools we have. Expectant as ever, Evan extended his hand yet again. "So are you gonna just give me a hard time, or are you gonna take my hand and let a guy introduce himself properly?"

Unexpected, however, was the retort, which came, not from Katherine, who just stared, but from across the bar.

"Cash only," Reuben gently admonished. "I can't show receipts after two o'clock. Y'all ain't even supposed to be up in here, but…"

"…but membership has its privileges," Katherine completed giggling, then, regarded the kid again in a sidelong glance that dropped a shock of red hair over her right eye, leaving the left one unobstructed to wink at Reuben. Dragging deep, she crossed her arms, exhaled languorously into the silence, and awaited an admission of penury from the boy in the pretty silk trousers.

Evan, obviously unsettled, and struggling to maintain his

game face, barely managed an "…uh" after a good fifteen seconds into this unforeseen glitch. Reuben drew a breath preparing to interject something characteristically face-saving, again, like a gentleman barman, or a warrior who had conflicts of far greater import to engage elsewhere, and could easily, in good heart, just let this thing go. But he was checked in that intention by just the slightest raise of the two fingers holding the cigarette in Katherine's right hand. She was enjoying her suitor's face just the way it was. It had her undivided attention as it flushed. And, had Evan ever known even a moment's exchange with Little Pete, he would have recognized that same stare that Katherine now leveled at him from beneath her burning brow. Consideration, perhaps almost empathy, cloaked in a veil of unapologizing unconcern a shade or two shy of disdain.

His face, more precisely his ability or inability to save it himself, was what she sat enigmatically scrutinizing in silence and cigarette smoke, hoping against hope that he might yet pull game enough out of his ass to arouse her.

"ATM?" he asked at last. And Katherine dropped her head forward to indulge a private chuckle, equal parts amusement and dismay at what all her prospective paramour had been able to come up with.

"It's three blocks down the street," Reuben replied empathetically, though not empathetically enough to refrain from adding with an involuntary chortle, "…in the pissin' rain…"

Katherine was tempted to let him run the three blocks in the deluge that had swallowed up the night just to see if he'd come back, knowing that Reuben wouldn't let him in again if he returned. But even penniless and arguably pathetic by old neighborhood standards, she reckoned, particularly on a wet night turning rapidly into a cold morning, he was of greater value in the hand than any assorted half dozen better men than he three blocks away bangin' on the bank wall for honest legal tender in the rain.

"Well now shit, Seamus, what good are you of a 3 A.M. without the first paper dollar to your name?"

To Evan, feeling slightly smaller in his suit, the question seemed loaded. And his customary hubris seemed suddenly an unwise choice in coloring his response. So he said nothing. He just grinned. And Katherine let him.

"I'll tell you what," Reuben offered far too appeasingly for Katherine's purposes, as if it weren't difficult enough to judge this boy's casual partner merits. "We'll call these on me, but then the bar's closed, cool?"

"No, Rube, that's completely unacceptable," Katherine interjected, intoning with sultry sovereignty. She took a long last drag and held it as she looked to the floor, dropping her butt and snuffing it beneath her shoe. Then, raising her eyes to consider both gentlemen once more on the lingering exhalation, she seemed to take inventory of the words she'd yet to speak. "There is no reason that *I* should have to stop drinkin' just because this broke-ass bon vivant doesn't have a quarter! This is exactly the way things get outta hand," she said, laughing through her language the way she did at three in the morning when liquor made her more honest about things than angry at them; more mischievous than malevolent. "You go see whatchu gotta do. I'm gonna have a speak with this fella, and I'm sure we can resolve this unfortunate little wrinkle in such a way as so nobody has to be deprived of their requisite overindulgence of alcohol, and, uh, things."

Reuben was much more economical with his smiles. Katherine was too. He wandered off down the bar with a slight backward glance and with only the faintest hint of a remote mirth playing across his full, fat lips and hers. Katherine threw back her drink and returned her attention to the boy who, despite his present troubles, and all her disparagement, seemed not to have been discouraged. He smiled yet again, or still, extending his hand to her once more, valiantly, as if something had changed for the better. And she shook her head.

"You know, Seamus, it distresses me how paper money seems to have gone the way of the handshake. It really doesn't mean anything anymore, does it?"

Evan was stalwart, holding out his hand, grinningly oblivious apparently to anything but his own ends. So Katherine continued.

"A handshake from a man who carries credit cards is as empty and worthless as the plastic that stands in for his money." That seemed to have degraded his overworked grin to a bemused smirk. "You want my hand? I'm flattered. But first we have to give your handshake some value. Okay," Katherine said as she reached for her clutch purse on the bartop, her voice never rising above the rough, smoky whisper it had been since midnight. "Now I'll tell ya, here's how this is gonna go. In my purse here I've got a roll of bills totaling five hundred dollars, which is the cash amount my father, God rest'm, always told me every self-respecting gentleman should carry on his person, an admonition which I have forever taken to heart. Ten percent of this sum, right here, right now, I give to you to put in your pocket. It is my gift to you in recognition of your attempt, albeit faltering, to be just such a self-respecting gentleman. Whichever pocket you choose is acceptable, though you being a right-handed fella as I was able to deduce from your tiresome propensity for extending it to me—somewhat flaccidly I might add—the right front pants pocket is recommended."

Speaking as if explaining matters of import to someone's six-year-old, she folded the bills once over and slapped them firmly into his still waiting palm. There was a nurturing quality to it, in both her demeanor and tone, disarming perhaps in her gentle condescension. Evan was no longer smiling, but nor was he clearly put off. Somewhere on the pleasant side of nonplussed he obediently if clumsily deposited the small wad of bills in the pocket of his slacks.

"Pleated pants, like these very ones that you are so handsomely modeling for us tonight, are good because the pockets are spacious, and they allow a fella with big, strong hands easy access to his ready cash, and, if I may emphasize the word 'strong' in reference to hands, may I also emphasize the word 'ready' in reference to cash."

Her reluctant pupil's hesitant tractability raised Katherine's pulse. She paused to be still and feel it, and to lick her lips, and to watch him waiting on her next word. "Now, mind you," she tutored on, "there is an entire etiquette to be observed concerning the taking out and putting away of large sums of paper money, and a man's facility with the proper motions and techniques can look affected and unnatural after he's been slingin' plastic for too long. But this is a whole 'nother set of issues, and these are perhaps lessons for another day when you have earned the privilege of knowin' me better. In the meantime…"

Reuben had materialized again as unobtrusively as he had just moments ago spirited himself away, this time proffering a pair of scissors which Katherine took from his hand without for an instant disturbing the hushed and lyrical rhythm of her diatribe.

"…in exchange for this manifold boon, I ask only that I be permitted to dispose of this inelegant abstraction of your value thusly." She had handily cut the thing in halves, quarters, and tossed the severed parts over her shoulder before she had even finished stating her intention, and certainly before Evan could have thought to have done something about it. Not that any part of Reuben's six-foot-five standing by suggested that he might have had the option to *do* much of anything at all. She waited in her dissertation. They all did. Katherine nearly breathless, anticipating the empty sound in the silence that the four plastic pieces of inanity made as they clattered to the linoleum floor. Then…

"Further, I would like most to secure from you a promise that you will never again do any woman, whom you would like to have seriously consider the potential of fucking you, the disrespect of thinking that your high-limit credit cards will be more impressive to her than your ability to lick your thumb, count off, and put down on the bar your hard earned dollars in an indirect exchange for some portion of her romantic attention. Agreed?"

Katherine accepted his slightly slack-jawed, vacant stare as acquiescence.

Continuing then, she counted and configured more paper money.

"Good. Now next, another fifty dollars I am going to put down here to cover the cost of these libations including a sizable gratuity for our handsome tapster."

Taking the once-folded fifty bones in her two fingers, she

waved them in front of the boy, then swept the bills twice across Reuben's waiting palm before closing hands with him across the bar. She held his hand too tightly and for too long for Evan to feel at all included.

Then, like an afterthought, "You're not one of these eighteen percenters on top of everything else, are you, Seamus? 'Cuz I hate those."

Evan knew himself to be, in fact, a generous tipper, and would have liked to have claimed at least as much, but assumed that the question was rhetorical in the scant space he was afforded to answer as Katherine kept on.

"And since I seem to recall that you were so magnanimously picking up the tab this evening, we'll call that fifty bucks you owe me. Now…if you place your hand into your right pocket you will immediately feel the comforting substance of the somewhat anemic though no less palpable roll of bills that you have secured there. It would now be a most opportune time to practice the withdrawal, the counting, and the *non*-virtual exchange of the fifty paper dollars that would ensue in the settling of the debt that you have incurred to me. Thereafter, you might far more legitimately extend to me that selfsame hand for the purposes of an introduction, with an equally legitimate expectation of a favorable response. Because, you see, *that* hand is the hand of another fella entirely. I can now take *this* man's hand in mine and get on with the no less important business of ascertaining many things beyond his most basic, but essential ability to keep a few quarters in his own kick."

Evan, not deftly, but with a focused attention to details as they had been explained to him, executed the maneuver. Nibbling his lower lip in concentration, he unfolded the fresh bills and counted to fifty in denominations of fives and tens. He fanned them out in his fingers like a hand of cards, an unexpected flourish from a neophyte that Katherine found both endearing and titillating, and he held them out to her in silence with a look of self-satisfaction spreading across his freckled mug.

She took the bills from his hand, letting their fingers touch, refolded them and returned them to her purse. Then she extended her hand into which he placed his, his smug façade giving way to smiling once again, broadly, like a child whose finger-painted masterpiece had just gained some long longed-for approval. Katherine introduced herself. She was not so apt to smile back at him, but even her speaking her name as she squeezed his hand had another color to it; one perhaps announcing, at length, her suddenly actual availability. The loud absence of callous in Evan's palms was not particularly arousing. Nor was the middling strength of grip with which he shook her hand. Katherine suspected it might be a holdover from the mating rituals that Evan's time in Hollywood and down below Soho had inclined him to observe. She thought to address it. She thought as well to further delineate the nuances that distinguished cash from credit, two divergent ideas of value that she was certain still had no lasting distinction one from the other in Evan's mind, and, in the moment, couldn't possibly matter to him nearly as much as fucking. But too many lessons presented all at once had proven intimidating to paramours in the past, even to the point of impacting performance. They were trivial matters under the circumstances, better left to the morning, considering there would certainly be a few others of a more utilitarian nature to be broached over the next several hours. Evan smiled to excess.

Katherine found it cute in an irritating sort of way, but wondered mostly if, for all his beauty, it was the best use he knew to make of his mouth.

Beth and Roman

R oman lay sprawled on his face about the bed, half-dreaming, less than half-awake, reached for her, his fingers finding, feeling the contour of an uncovered hip, his touch her stirring, turning from him, a long, irregular breath, exhaling, pressing her back against him, and he wishing he could be outside of himself on mornings like these; outside of himself, invisible, and watching the two of them together, waking, and behaving like two do when their only acquaintance has been made by the trial and error of an unplanned, first-time tryst; when the light of the morning reveals that they are beautiful.

It was a thing to be viewed from the ceiling, looking down at them, in order to have been appreciated fully, the blossoming out of sleep into ownership of what they'd done, and the winsome combination of want and worry within it. Unposed, awakening strangers, spellbound, tentative, a little each wondering if the other will make the next moment unlovely somehow with some involuntary impulse of their real, daylight lives, their daylight selves. But the new moments arrive and go past, and neither does, and the bed smells like the commingled sweat and fragrances of them, and neither have smelled it before, and they are confused by it, overcome, awestruck by all of the senses playing wickedly with them in a dream on the edge of sleep. Eyes open and they look, she back over her shoulder and up, he raised up on an elbow and down, and then they close, just effort enough, more, moment by moment, of comfort coming on and receding concern, and down. Down into all is well. Wholly well. Healthily well. Down into perfectly, peacefully, nakedly, unbreakably well...

He kissed her hipbone, or consumed it, covered it entirely where it was so obviously waiting, with his mouth. Her body shook, and he collapsed back onto his face. An arm left draped she took and pulled tight around her ribs, and held it hard to her, a strong, little fist, holding him by the wrist, between tiny breasts, and slept again. He heard it in the slowing rhythm of her breaths, and felt her grip grow easy.

Their sex, if he were recalling correctly back through the viscosity of night and sleep, had been like Moscato D'asti and the Kahlua cheesecake he had shared with her at dinner. Delicious and decadent, sinful, leaving him feeling as though he should reproach himself for his gluttony, even as the very act and taste and sacred effervescence of it made his entire body tremble still like that, like her, and be joyful, and perfectly, peacefully well.

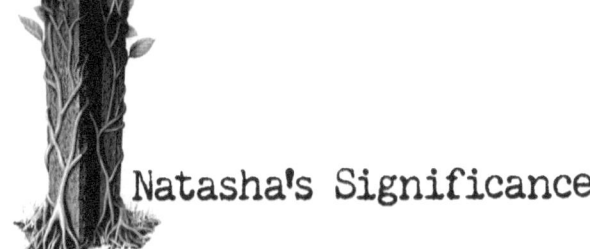Natasha's Significance

Natasha was still a week from returning. Mostly in the mornings, as there was always time to misspend then, over coffee Danny Ezra reflected on how he should receive her.

They would not speak that coming week, and had not spoken for days before. Because somewhere in the weeks past, words had taken up the space that being was in, and, for his taste, silence was better. Silence was rife with all the as yet unchosen realities waiting to blossom, like the time before they'd met. There were no words between them then, just the forces that the Earth in its orbit imposed, and the surrendering to them that animals do. Then people begin to attempt to mitigate and manipulate those forces with intellect, and Ezra, striving to preserve the innate, had refused to play at that, both in deed, and, he'd thought, in plain old English as well.

Now, at the seat of his musing, since they'd seen one another last, was an awareness of a reluctance on both their parts to *act* in whole truths; to evince nakedly, each in plain view of the other, and themselves, "This is who I am. Moreover, this is what I will never truly be myself in your presence without." And this reluctance, if not soon corrected, he mused, promised to leave them both with so muddled a cognition of the other as to be worthless for the purpose of founding a relationship upon. Not corrected, he thought further, but removed, and replaced by the *behaving* their truths as opposed to this late testifying to them in cold conference. As it had been at first.

"You know," he said to her, one of the last things he'd said when they'd parted, standing curbside at the airport with a sickened air between them, holding before he spoke at the top of his breath to rein in his tone, "There is hardly a single word that ever means precisely the same thing to any two people. Ever… You do know that, yes?"

It had seemed to him that they had come so gorgeously naked into one another's presence at first, so unabashedly who they were as beasts, that from the present place Ezra could only recall it as a dream state. He wanted a return to it.

There was nothing wrong with the distance between them, nor the time between their time together. But if any lasting partnership of his was to be explored in such a context, it would need to be built upon a re-establishment of the absolutes that had gotten them dreaming to begin with. And the dreams, each their own, that had caused them to materialize in the presence and plain sight of one another, and be recognized. The way they had forgotten to greet each other when they'd first met, or engage in small talk; someone telling a story about somebody's King Charles Spaniel, or someone's last job, or discovering that they liked the same wine, jokes that weren't funny, and sundry other declarations of "I am." The way that their indwelling imperatives spoke to one another, ignoring their rational selves as though they were children to be seen and not heard.

This morning, it were as if their human aspects had, at some point after the first three months, suddenly realized that they were people, and that they should perhaps discuss some things, and they were awakened, and devolved into "a couple" with concerns that needed now to be aired and considered. It were as if perhaps their most basic inclinations flowing together so fiercely had scared them by colluding, despite their practical guides, in behaviors that they would not be able to explain to the culture they would ultimately need to go out and function in.

Somewhere, suddenly, that explanation had become a matter of regard. Something besides *them* had become answerable. Inexplicably. And now there was oddity in their distance. There was uncertainty in the space and time between them. There were surmises, tonalities misconstrued, misremembering of things that had been, and anxiety, like a subtle stench in the air, over how things would go forth…

It was no one's fault. In those embryonic, chemically induced states of new romance, it is easy to float for a while in an amniotic fluid of pheromones and endorphins. Easy if lovers are not busy apologizing for, or denying altogether, being driven by powers that lead from their groins, not from their heads, and certainly not from their hearts… Just say nothing, and let your most primal, most animal beauty conduct you. There is a challenge in that which they had risen to, to have spent their first six or seven encounters in silence, with nothing in between but the physical magnetism, trusting to its fearsome potency to incite them to more and further coming together, and offering it no resistance. To have walked in silence throughout the intervals between their trysts, whether together or apart with no yammer of plans, or aspirations, or extended families, or long stories of lives past turned mythology upon which all the future should be based, all the anti-arousal of expectation letting instead every apprehension lie struck down in the path of their rabid passions that frightened, but in as equal a measure compelled them to *be* first, and *be* fully.

They had reaped the rewards of their bravery in ecstasies so profound that surely, Ezra suspected, they remained as ghosts in the rooms where they had so unrestrainedly, and unrelentingly conjoined. Certainly the sounds and smells, and other sensory fallout of their rapture resided still, faint whispers of having been, between the floorboards, beneath the beds, in the ceiling corners of the rooms. So much so that he would imagine others coming after saying, "There is something pervades this place that is utterly carnal. There is no other way to describe it. The air is wet with passion. Lust here is the presiding emotion." He hoped those lingering energies left in their wake would exhort others to abandon compromise and the mediocrity it bred.

But how fogged delineations and designations become in the sticky morass of romantic parlance once it begins, as it is that most lovers know no truths with regard to themselves, but only that which they have unknowingly made up based upon the preponderance of the equally erroneous data around them. They have taken from the common design of what a romance is, and called it their own.

"Most people don't do things the way you do, Ezra," his last lover had wept loudly at him during their last conversation bent on "saving" the relationship.

"Being a part of 'most' is nothing to be proud of, you simple little cunt!" he'd spat back as a final retort, despising her tears that fell in lament for her pedestrian needs; a waste of passion in a useless conflict of words and raised voices, indicting him *and* his relationship as fraudulent, and making him ashamed. Despite his adamance, the vernacular of "most" would follow him, his self-perceptions, like everyone's, tinged by thoughts of how "others are."

And he was crestfallen considering how it, this same vernacular, had sprung up like weeds in a freshly flowering garden between Natasha and him; in language cloaked as communication, insidiously thrusting the onus of self-validation for each onto the other, so that instead of being what they were, they had begun to say, in sentences designed for safety, "This is how I want *your* behavior to allow me to view myself." And how often do lovers, at least one of them in a pair, on the futile search for the definitive coupling, thinking such is synonymous with self-worth, get up to this in the dialect of debtors and creditors, instead of letting their sensual creatures preside, who know nothing of gift and receipt, but only that to which nature compels, and for which it rewards them?

Where had their bravery gone? Ezra thought back on the last month of them together and apart, of half-talk and half-truth and was disappointed with himself for having ever indulged it. For such relationships, he thought, deserved to be nothing, to be lived in compromise until, like all common things, they faded away down some too well-trod path of perpetual concession.

In Vancouver they had come together several months before, at the very beginning, during that data gathering time of first dates, or whatever, where negotiations, for "most people," advance under any number of different names, like "seeing each other," and "going out." The mornings brought the cold, fat fog, full of intention, and momentum, rolling in off of English Bay. From some high story window at the hotel whose name was lost in his memory they watched it march towards them over the tops of the surrounding buildings. Natasha, wrapped in a blanket, then wrapped in him, was silent looking from the window in the stillness, feeling him behind her clutching strongly to her nakedness with what she had already come to recognize as his proprietary embrace. There seemed nothing more organic to them then; he extending a hand for her and she reaching up to take it without a word, instinctively, because it had been extended; he pulling her naked from the bed and dragging the blanket after, wrapping it around her at the window, though not before stopping at an observer's distance, far enough to take in the all of her standing there, far enough to define his place and hers, to watch her wait for him, exposed to him within and to the world without, and cold, for a duration he imposed and she endured; they then standing there together, unspoken, until room service knocked.

It had several sounds. They heard the elevator first. Then the trundling of a cart along the carpeted hallway. Then that particular knock which, like the fog, and other things that didn't lie, came inevitably, and was also full of intention. Another presence in the room changed everything. Though briefly that presence remained, energetically it was long enough to create a whole new way of things…for whose benefit? Mightn't they have maintained the manifest properties eagerly surfacing of unspoken orders and silent, willing acquiescence if they had owned them outright? Or did the intrusion of a stranger force an equalizing of the atmosphere that caused the coalescing couple, as if caught misbehaving, to slip almost inadvertently into forms "most" would recognize of normalness, and representative parity? Would the world outside the suite do that to them?

A wordless hour over coffee would pass before they found their way back to the unlearned symbiosis that they had awakened in. An hour, and then Ezra, after buttering the broken half of a croissant with his finger, lifted his hand to Natasha's face without looking up, and she, without looking up, took the finger between her lips and sucked it clean. Then he looked…then she, and toward the floor again.

By the time she arrived to be with him in San Francisco, *her* knock had since become distinct as well. His first morning above another inviting and gloomy city, he had risen early in anticipation, his head hurting from dousing the intensity of his impatience for her late into the night before in the hotel bar. Room service had already knocked. "Coffee for you, sir," the sound of that knock said before the man's voice did. (He was always generous with room service staff. Although he was buying their respect, he appreciated why they would, really rather cheaply, put it up for sale. "Most" people sell their submission for a dollar amount, because money is always needed, and it is the only thing that one always has that they can sell. "Most" others purchase their dominance. And in most cases, having no tools to explore it beyond the anemic set of notions that most are born into and have lived their lives upon, are contented with the false submission that money buys them.) The middle-aged porter literally bowed at the waist for the ten dollars he was handed, and walked out backward through the door that Ezra held open all smiles and obeisance. Ezra smiled as well, thinking how, if the man had done that which he'd just for free, "most" would call it "kink." But what if—killing time he stood drifting through his caffeine-fueled reflections—what if servility were, in fact, his soul-labeling? What if his practiced obsequiousness, from the moment he entered the room through the moment of his dismissal, was not at all for the purpose of eliciting a gener-ous remuneration? What if his smile was not bought, the way so many are, but all of his deferential attention, impeccably and to the utmost applied, even in the simple task of delivering and pouring the first morning coffee, was offered up in gratitude of being let do that wherein his spirit was most freely manifest? What if the room servant's knock anticipated that someone, anyone on the other side of the door, because they were there, because they had called, held out to him salvation; with not even a nickel ever changing hands held out to him a circumstance that "most" would accept—all the arbiters of the aberrant beyond the little room—for him to unabashedly indulge his nature; to be who he was?

Trying to shake off some piece of a cold that had found its way into his sinuses, he wandered about the spacious suite with coffee cup, eager for her, achy and touch deprived.

Something about hotel rooms. A bed, a bathroom, perhaps a table and a couple of chairs…an armoire or dresser of some sort. The set dressing of a simple hiding place. And then, lovers fill the generic space with sounds and scents…well…to start at the beginning…

She knocked on the door. It could have been no one else's knock. Faint, four knocks distinctly, two, softly and rapid, and then a pause, like a space to contemplate commitment in, then two again but slower, as if less certain, breaking the silence in the room too high above the ground for street sounds to penetrate, confessing some things. When had she made those her sounds? When had he come to recognize them as such? They had shown one another their most essential selves, elements that they could not now un-show. He bit and raised welts, took with hands strong with intention, and without regard for the sanctity of anything once called "private," held, lifted, tossed her by the throat and the pubis. She wore his hands where they led her, spread her, wore his mouth where it sought out the taste of each separate part of her, wore his cum upon her heaving chest and in her hair with proud pants of achievement, not surrendering to his dominance so much as rising to her own submission, taking him to task, and wearing him, ultimately, to sleep. And now, this morning, she was returning. This morning she was back, and her soft, signature knock reiterated, "I'm here, and I've come to make good. I've come to *be* good. It *is* good, how I've come." For all that, it was just a knock. Though any and all that came after could not have come had Ezra not heard it for what it was. Or if she had pounded hard, with insistence, leaving him no room to accept her, no space to be the benevolent dictator on the other side of the door. Or if she had not come at all.

A lot can happen just on the inside of a hotel suite door after the sounds of the door itself, unlocking, opening, closing, and locking again behind the entrant—the noises of commit-ment—have gone to ghost. There in the little shadowed alcove that was then filled with them, and the smell of her hair, and the soap she bathed with, his slight stink, the sweat of a restless sleep and the past night's indulgence... First contact can go so many ways depending upon mood, or need, one would suppose. Kissing and breathing...new sounds in the silence. Whispering, giggling, sighing. And the rustle of clothing there in that tight little space. All very distinct, as are "strip me slowly" kinds of sounds, as opposed to the "I can't get naked fast enough, quit the bullshit and fuck me hard" variety. And yet, she was predictable in this, their latest confluence, as was he. Such types of couples make particular sounds when they meet. Such animals do not tend to find themselves just inside hotel suite doors, trembling with arousal unless it is the arousal of certitude, the audible coursing of anticipation; anticipating that demands are most certainly about to be brought, and just as certainly answered.

The shifting of them and their garments—Ezra had on his half-buttoned jeans beneath a hotel robe, and the open belt buckle made a constant tinkling echo as they moved in the warm, wet air around them—was punctuated at intervals by the quiet pop of a button, the metallic raspy whisper of a zipper, and the myriad huffs and titters clothing makes as it is dropped to the floor.

And then he stepped back to look at her standing in the alcove in nothing, saying nothing amidst a pile of baggage and cloth. She looked at the floor. If he went to her, placing one hand firmly on the nape of her neck and the other he pressed just as firmly against her pubic bone and squeezed, he was without doubt that every sound in the alcove would change, giving new ghosts rise. He did. They did. He laughed. She breathed. Natasha was naked. And warm. He had his hands on her, his right hand holding too tightly to her to suggest anything less than ownership. He was biting on her lower lip at the front end of a long, fat kiss, his other hand, grasping the nape of her neck, holding her mouth on his, ensuring without need that he was left at liberty to kiss her as fat and as long as his intent, for the moment, perhaps forever.

Natasha's body shuddered, as though the last currents of self-rule were passing from her through his two hands where they held her with such resolve, and from her mouth to his; shuddered as though he were taking them, and as though there were in her a tense but flagging struggle to remain the master of them. And then he would have no such struggle any longer, and had she a problem with that, she never would have knocked.

Ezra sat troubling over his cup at his kitchen table looking out over the misted Santa Monica Mountains, struggling to discern precisely when the wiggle words had begun to insinuate themselves, or if, had he recognized them at the precise moment she first uttered one, would he have taken the initiative to slap her. Apparently not, he ruminated. At some point he had become aware, and in his awareness, his first tendency had been to appease, which had led him to where he sat.

The sun was beginning to burn off the morning marine layer that the Angelinos had come to know as "June Gloom." In Los Angeles, even the fog was a liar. The coffee had grown cold. And there were morning calls that needed to be made.

Ezra stood, stretched, and went to find the shower, thinking, when Natasha returned...*if* she returned, he would abide no resumption of that non-committal discourse which *was* commitment for the unsure and confused. He thought it, but he knew no way back into nakedness and spontaneity. Like awakened Adam and Eve in the garden, how do you return? He couldn't take what was no longer being unreservedly offered. There could never be true jurisdiction over ill-defined dominion.

But no, he thought. She never would have knocked.

Natasha sat at a sidewalk table slowly spinning her demitasse cup on its saucer with her thumb and second finger. It was her fourth, and it was half a day already gone when she realized that she'd done nothing but twirl that cup and wander through recollections of the restaurant on the first evening.

How they'd eaten little but said nearly nothing. And how,

even in that precarious, preliminary space, to her own horror, she'd been compelled by such imperatives as she had, such as are governed only in the acquiescence, to part her lips when she saw him dip his middle finger into his snifter. How she sat then demurely, waiting, mouth open, like any trusting baby bird. How he had fed her that finger then, coated with anisette, just barely lifting his eyes to watch her receive it, as if knowing he needn't attend it further. And how she, as if needing to offer him the utmost assurance of such, took it, with a hunger and a gratitude; with a desire so intense to receive it, to please him, wordlessly confessing such blatant submission that he could have easily, carelessly exploited her nakedness. And how he didn't then, for such would have required thought; a sense of agenda, like the stuff of her own mental machinations that would later intrude, but instead he gave it no further regard, made no point of it, returned his attention to quaffing the contents of his snifter as though there were nothing more relevant to the present moment to consider... As though in this world where they came together there was nothing so obvious, and as though there would be no end of time to make use of her whensoever the best use she could be was the next most obvious thing that occurred to them both.

What had she been trying to achieve when later she began to question? They were thoughtless in the beginning. Or was that how it had been at all? It made no sense from a distance, or as the demands of daily business encroached and needed, themselves, to be controlled. It only made sense as a daydream, recurrent, and so vivid as to make her blush for no one but the waiter. And then the memory of this last language-tainted interim would rudely wake her. She'd asked questions that appeared to her, from the place she sat now, as the height of inanity, like "What does this mean?" and "What are we doing?" She'd used phrases to precede them, justifiers, like, "In practical terms…" as though everything could be, *should* be made, upon a say-so, practical…justifiable to some cumulative, common, barren and dreamless mind.

"Words will fail us," he had said finally, after attempting to honor insoluble questions with credible answers. "They fail everyone," he said with a sound like sorrowful admonition in his voice that she had never heard, staring her down with a disappointment in his face so solemn that it had made her look to the floor. He had called upon them anyway, the words, answering to her power play; answering to her choice to betray spontaneity and authenticity with the discourses of the common and cowardly, desiring to meet *her* need; desiring that *she* be pleased. And she had shown herself irresponsible, unready to wield such power, possessed of nothing to wield it for but the hollow victory of being able to say she had some say, unworthy to have such a one at her feet, where, from the moment he met her, he had been… Frightened by who she was and who he was, she had tried to speak as someone else in hopes that someone else would respond. And someone else did. It was her fault. She had made it less than it was. Asking, because some imposter of an inner voice had urged the inquiry, knowing no satisfactory rejoinder could result (satisfying what?), she had made that beginning time seem now so far away and unreal. No longer the spirits stirred by their animal familiars, she had raised the specter of doubt to haunt the turned uneasy air, leaving him to do battle with the question of what made her happy because she was afraid to fight with it, or, simply surrender to it, herself. Now he was conscious, and it was her fault.

A week away from where she sat with coffee on the Manhattan street, bustling with the rest of life's dilettantes and dabblers, she would go and stand outside his door, knock two times, and two times again, and hope, even though the odds from the present distance seemed remote, that he'd let her in. He should not, she thought. It would serve her right.

Kindness,
    Bobby,
    and Madeleine

Madeleine met me near the corner of 47th Street. I called her cell phone as I drove up Tenth Avenue saying, "Where are you?" and she said, "I'm just leaving this bar where I met my friend. I'm walking on Tenth between I don't know and I don't know. Where are *you*?" And I looked to the left, and there she was, walking along in this pair of pretty, pretty, beige heels (What is it with how the older I get the more I appreciate women's shoes?) made of wicker, or hemp, some sort of refined rustic like that, that were tied up around her ankles with gauzy fabric-like sandals. And she had on a short little, light-colored skirt that puffed out around her legs above mid-thigh. I don't know what you call those besides "cute." And some little top, not much more than a T-shirt as I recall. I remember it was a tiny thing, too small to hide a bra under. And so I remember thinking it was so sad how our women, they feel they've got to make boobs out of their breasts, because heaven help you if you've got small tits, but hide those nipples, so as to fuck up some divine, natural shape, tastefully covered in cotton, because, repressed as we are, God forbid we see a pair of braless titties through a tank top we lose our fucking minds. It's all so stupid. She never had breasts enough to need support for, little and perfect the way they were. But what are you going to do? Bras are, what, compulsory... Anyway... I remember the figure she cut, walking there on the avenue, how those shoes pronounced her calves. And I remember her bare arms and legs, as I threw open the passenger-side door and hollered, "Baby!" and all her skin of freckles, and freckles, and more pretty freckles she wasn't trying to hide. I remember her short, curly orange-blonde hair looking maybe like she'd just had it done. But mostly I remember how, for all that cute and girly, she hoisted her sweet little body up into the dirty cab of the truck with so much more purpose than pretense, like she was one of my boys hitching a ride to the grocery store, then leaned across to kiss me, smelling like original Carolina Herrera. I love that shit. That smell, that tuberose and whatever whatever they do, put me right back where I was the first time I smelled her, in the first place where I remember that her bravery made me want her, even though it might have been, not bravery at all, but stupidity, or mental illness. But trust is so arousing, isn't it? Trust, you know, maybe not in people, but in moments… Or honesty, like when she said back then, "I want to give you my number, but I'm chicken…" That was honest. *That* seduced me. So when she said, as we were passing 68th Street getting ready to get onto the West Side Highway, "Please don't be a serial killer…" it   sounded obligatory, a due diligence, like her bra, as if she needed me to know that she hoped that I knew that she knew that this was highly irregular. It was honest. Perfunctorily informing me that she knew that we knew each other for five minutes on the other coast, and that it had been two years since we'd seen one another, in which time we might have spoken twice, and now she was driving home with me, alone, to inevitably be naked, and fucking. We had spoken about it four times on the phone that day, and never once said the words, any of the words that explicitly express it, but even her first call to me that morning, to tell me, "Hey you! I'm in New York!" had said it. And she might have had a prettier word to paint a prettier picture of it now, but the picture was pretty enough from where I sat. And from where she sat, I think, too, or she wouldn't have chosen to be in it, that picture, I mean, fuck, we're beautiful, right? Just so beautiful, beautiful this thing we make, this thing we do, we people, beautiful. But it was irregular, and she needed me to know, or to know that she knew. To know that *I* was irregular; that what she had for me, and had held for me for two years that would make her meet a near stranger on a Manhattan street corner and get into his truck and let him drive her off to points unknown, take off her clothes and put his dick in her, was extraordinary, and what a damned shame if it was all a mistake and she ended up with a communicable disease or dead, and doubted she would, but had to say something that expressed to me that she hoped that I knew that she knew. Honesty. And again, that seduced me. And there was nothing for me to say back… A serial killer isn't going to say, "Yeah, sorry, I'm one of those." Or somebody isn't going to share their contemplation about how they've got venereal warts, but hey, they just really want to fuck you. So I didn't much see the point in saying anything, about that, or about how I'd like to slap the motherfucker that taught her that she needed to hide and/or manipulate her pretty little breasts with some device. And that was the last I heard of it. We talked all the ride home about other stuff. About how we'd been, and who we were. We laughed out loud, navigating the nerves with an underscore courtesy of WBGO, and pulled up at about a quarter to ten in front of Sarandakos Gyro, where Bobby Sarandakos was standing outside with a cigarette, looking tired and easy that the day was over, and watching me pull into the "no standing" zone. I asked Madeleine to stay in the truck and drive it around the block if a cop came. She told me that'd be no problem…like a boy… Once I got out, and stood still, and could look back through the door across the driver's seat at her, under the streetlights, I could pay full attention to her looking like a package on the passenger seat that somebody wrapped up in ribbons and pretty paper. And I thought, Who the fuck am I that this painfully lovely child should trust me, or trust now? I ain't that brave, and I don't much deserve people who are; lovely, fine-ass people, naked, up next to me, smellin' like original Carolina Herrera. And that's what I kept right on thinking as I jog-skipped halfway up the block to the Greek place, and Bobby, like a big, tired warrior, gave me a hug, and a kiss on the cheek, and said, "Who is that?" and I said, "That's Madeleine." And that was it. He had it all figured out. I could see him taking a second to put it together, looking past me down at the flashing taillights of the truck. I looked too, and I saw her sitting there through the rear window, and I wondered what she was thinking, hoping it was something like, I must be crazy… I must be stupid, or crazy, or both, but this boy's clearly got some love in him and I want him to hand it over. And I looked back at Bobby. And he snuffed his cigarette under his foot like he knew something and said, "Whadya need?"

"We need some food," I said. So we went inside, and I got some calamari and the best goddamn pea soup on the planet.

Bobby said, "You want wine?'

And I said, "I think I got some at home."

And he said, with his arm already in the refrigerator, "Just take this… White? Red…? Here, take white." His big, square frame moving around the tiny place, quicker than usual, in between tables, over to the serving counter, moving chairs out of the way, over to the beverage fridge. Not a lot ever played in his face, but when he moved, love and mischief in collusion, you know how they do, made him faster, and a little frenetic. "You want some baklava…?"

And I said, "Nah," but he'd already taken enough baklava out of the tray to feed dessert to half a dozen people and was wrapping it all up.

"What else?" he said as he handed me the bag and hugged me again. And I was coming from my pocket, but he said, "Nah, just go."

And I said, "You sure…?"

And he said, "Always with the freckles, huh?"

And I had to laugh. I stood there and I laughed, a little astounded. A lot astounded. It was a night to be astounded in… Full of only the loveliest of things…

And I said, "You could see that from where you were standin'?"

And he said, "I guessed. Go on. Don't keep her waitin'."

And I jog-skipped back down the street. Like a fucking six-year-old…

Climbing into the truck, I handed the bag across the cab to Madeleine. She looked over at me, and I watched her eyes looking at the way the parts of my face moved as I said, "My boy Bobby thinks you're lovely, and he gave us all this food, because he saw you, and he just wants me to be happy, and how could you not make me happy being you, and being this thing, and lookin' like you do, trusting me, which he saw?"

We drove home and I ran my mouth all the way about how just a little kindness can make so much change, and about how it's easy to be kind if we're not afraid. It was full-heartedness, all that language, one part gratitude, one part simple pleasure, distilled joy, so fuckin' elusive, and one more part nervous anticipation of seeing her naked except for those sexy, nouveau-rustic, beige high-heeled sandals.

When I came up tight behind her in my little kitchen while she was dishing up the food, she was simple about it. She was still, and compliant, me lifting her curls out of the way to take a bite out of the back of her neck. She planted her hands on the countertop among the open containers, spread her legs a little bit, and planted her feet, dropped her head forward and offered me all of it, like, "Whatever you're bringin', bring it, Boss. I'm down." But she said, very softly, "You're obviously hungry, so why don't we eat?" So we cleared some space in my cluttered living room, and ate on our laps, and didn't say much.

I spent a long time lying close beside her on the bed, trying to act all nonchalant with her nakedness and freckles and fooling, I think, nobody.

I don't know how long I must have lain there playing with the distances from which the warmth coming up off of her skin and the faint traces of Carolina Herrera could still hit me in the face.

And staring at the shadow of a bird with wings spread that someone had carved out of the finest remnant of yellow-red hair on the crest of her pubic bone. It looked like a dusting of colored confectioner's sugar stenciled on a cupcake.

I think I eventually let her take those shoes off too.

—For Caroline, Summer 2010

Andre
and
Elaine

Elaine waited at the gate for the gunmetal gray sedan to roll up the road and come to stop at the foot of the drive. Standing like an anticipatory statue in the fading light of the evening she waited and watched the crest of the road where any moment it would come gliding into view. Andre had phoned at 4:30 saying he would come for her at 6. And she waited, eager to see and be with him.

"Wear black," he had specified. "Choose nicely for me. No jewelry. Nothing can make you more beautiful. Just wear black. Except for the gloves. I prefer the green gloves."

Green?! What green gloves? she had thought, and would have immediately voiced if the phone hadn't gone dead. Instead, Elaine inhaled deeply as if oxygen could extinguish conflicting emotion, and hung up. She stood there by the bedside table breathing in awarenesses. Her man was an asshole, that was one; a willful, exasperating, self-interested asshole. She breathed that in, exhaled, and breathed in another; that he was a glorious asshole, who knew his child's heart and spoke his man's desires in terms often far too ingenuously comingled to be left un-adored. He was a clown, like the ones that would scare children at the circus, rather than make them laugh, because it was evident, even to a child, that their notions could always possibly be danger-ous, and could hurt. He was a boy who might be enthralled to watch the butterfly crawl around on his finger's end, or pin its wings to the wall, as equally fascinated with its struggle to get free. She breathed *that* deeply. An articulate egotist who could discern fact from fantasy with an unmerciful intellect while maneuvering like a clever coward always somewhere between the two. Her arrogant hero whose delicate muses she guarded with a fierceness far surpassing any she reserved for her own use, and whose flights of fancy, if she did not fly with them, she indulged for a vicious love's sake. She breathed that joyous melancholy, its arousing confusion, there by the bedside standing, and then went to run the bath.

Leaving her tub to fill, Elaine went to roam her closets for what would please him. A quarter of an hour passed in the finding and laying out of her evening clothes; a backless gown, a pair of garter-less stockings. Perhaps as a matter of protocol, from a drawer, she selected a lacey black thong and left it lying on the dresser top. Then back to the bath to turn off the tap. Then back again to find shoes and earrings, and deep in some other drawer, buried and forgotten, like the masquerade party they'd been purchased for, a pair of long green satin gloves. She pulled them out and laid them with the rest. Had he taken an uninvited inventory once, and remembered, locked them away, the green gloves, in the cabinet of his diabolical little brain? Of course he had. And there it all lay across the bed, a fatal ensemble, but for some game of his, almost entirely in black.

Then, returning to the bath only to discover that the water had grown tepid in her wandering, and that the time she had taken had left her too pressed to reheat it, or to give her bathing any degree of the ceremony she required of it and would've otherwise been afforded, she stood on the tessellated floor lightly pounding upon it with her bare right foot and breathing a familiar frustration. She climbed into the disagreeable tub and quickly planted herself breast deep in the lukewarm water. She sat in it shaving her legs fitfully, unsatisfied, annoyed, and not needing to search far for reasons to curse the Prince. When she stood to rinse herself off she loitered beneath the shower, the cascade hotter and sympathetic, luxuriating in her perturbed and pensive mood. Raking her fingers through her finely groomed patch of pubic hair, she thought such things as how perhaps it would serve him right were she ten minutes late for taking the time to masturbate with the shower massage. She would have perhaps, were she even remotely motivated, and not simply searching for ways to spite him and his green gloves. Standing there beneath the stream, she half tried and vainly. Arousal was unsustainable with the recurrent image intruding of the attire she had chosen so deliberately, with an eye specifically for what she knew to be Andre's taste, and the Halloween costume ridiculous sort of wrong that green gloves were. And what was more, Andre knew they were.

His preference, as was often the case, was not really a preference at all, but rather one of many little arbitrary impositions that fed his ego when she would concede to them, and fueled the melodrama of his indignation when, infrequently, she would not. It was always more than a simple decision to go against his wishes. It was an intricate negotiation theirs, a delicate arbitrament that could not be efficiently executed by any but the enlightened, and insanely in love.

On her part, it required a majestic strength of will that she be contented never to wear on her sleeve. She would instead forever be the master in slave's clothing; the goddess in striking black, oddly adorned in leaf-green gloves, looking to others like the eccentric, they never aware that she was simply, valiantly, the obedient. For him, she would do that and more, inviting his authority, desiring he do his good pleasure, and use her however he saw most fit. And yet, better on occasion to disobey him outright and navigate the consequence, than ever allow him to firmly believe that pleasing his Lordship, while one of her utmost pleasures, was her *only* pleasure. Even the Master must be taught by example. She stepped from the tub and began to dry her hair. She had made some choices by the time she left the bathroom to go and dress that most might've called obvious. For her though, they required the entirety of that hour before she was to present herself to him. They required all of it.

She knew that Andre would have had it no other way. Well, perhaps he might have, at times, and for moments. But, in two years of knowing him, she had come to recognize and trust that he ultimately understood some things that most men, in her experience, generally didn't. Ostensibly realizing that power, for the most part, was not his, but resided with the woman, he had shown himself prepared to get nearer to it through thoughtful dialogue and gentle, benevolent guile than through all ham fisted efforts else. Ham-fisted he had as well... Or fisted, at least... His chiseled hands, she saw as tools as much for roughly gathering up her hair in, or closing around her throat when he held her against the wall to kiss her, as for, say, playing the piano, which he did as well when she asked him to, and if she made sure to effuse adoration during his performance. But just as often he seemed nearly to admire that the other species granted him audience at best; that he was a perennial guest at the feminine feast, but that being invited to eat depended entirely upon the art of his table manners. Still Andre, even while basking, as he did, in his mistress' nearness with the utmost appreciation, guarded his fragile machismo without apology, and with innately masculine pride, and *she* understood that this too was endemic and a birthright. To her, this conglomerate that he was of complex sensibilities, all inextricably fierceness and fragility, was irresistible. Her invitations to come and eat, given beauty, his watchful patience, and his own unhurried, inferior, but masterfully conjured magic, could quickly become her imploration to be fed. He knew it, and she knew he knew it. Elaine often thought that Andre would've made a rather formidable woman as well.

She sat naked at her dressing table dallying with make-up that she didn't really need. If she was as self-possessed, she was not quite so self-aware as he was, and she enhanced her eyes and her lips mostly to honor his sense of having been prepared for. As she applied her eyeliner in the mirror, she glanced now and again at the clock, and over her shoulder where she could feel Andre's eyes at her back, and hear the sound of his breathing. While she knew she would not find him standing there, so strongly now had he come to saturate her sphere that she looked for him just the same, matter-of-factly. Even after confirming his absence she would continue to scan the room behind her reflected in the mirror without regret or expectation, but simply because.

"Tell me the story of the falcon again, Andreas," she said as she touched her throat and traced a line with a perfume soaked finger down to her navel.

"Is it the story of the falcon?" His voice was fluid and deep, and wafted over her shoulders like incense smoke. "Or the story of the falconer?"

"We've never quite made that determination, have we?" she said chuckling.

"We've made it many times," he said, having to chortle almost tiredly at the thought himself.

"Just tell it," she said. His laugh caressed the back of her neck and brought the smell of him to the room.

"Well, as you know, the falcon is like no other animal, nor is it like any other bird for that matter. Strictly speaking, it can't ever be truly domesticated. There is simply an agreement of sorts between itself and the artful falconer wherein…"

"Why is he an artful falconer and she not an artful falcon?"

"Well what I am trying to illustrate is that…"

"I know what you're trying to illustrate, Andre. I know this story. I just think…"

"The artful falcon then! The lovely, glorious, beguiling, artful fucking falcon." Elaine laughed out loud, glanced behind her in the mirror and returned to mascara and lip liner.

"That's all very flattering," she said, "but really she just is what she is, isn't she?"

"My point exactly," he said.

"I know," she replied. "Tell the story."

"The falconer will entice—"

"Persuade."

"…persuade the bird to be his—"

"In appearance."

"Yes, in appearance, by convincing her—"

"By their mutually concluding…"

"I'll spank you, Elaine! So help me, I'll beat your fat ass!"

"I haven't a doubt, Andre," Elaine said, poorly suppressing her laughter. "I would expect nothing less. I'm sorry."

"No you're not."

"I am," she said. "Truly... Forgive me."

Andre was silent, and Elaine in the mirror forced herself to suppress any expression of concern that her insolence might have driven him from the room. But soon again she heard him, his measured dissertation, as if having stopped to re-collect his disheveled authority and now begun again. And she tried to only listen; to wallow in the sound of him and not react in words to what he was saying. It was easy to steep herself in Andre...and not.

"...The falconer will persuade the bird to be his—in appearance—via their mutual agreement that there is a benefit for her in being owned."

"And for him in ownership," she failed miserably to refrain from interjecting.

"Of course," Andre allowed, tightly. "And yet, what does he ever actually own? Unless he is going to keep her in a cage, which has no value to either party, he has to let her fly. And once she is free of his glove, he has no control over the choices she makes. If she chooses to fly away, he can only call to her and follow until she decides to return to him, if in fact she ever does. It is to that end, and purely for his sake that she makes her biggest sacrifice. She agrees to be fitted with little bells, secured to her leg, so that she can be heard and tracked when she is out of his hand. But more than that, it is his mark to which she acquiesces; an audible, attention drawing symbol of her captivity."

"Not any more, Andre, what with radio telemetry, GPS these

days and all that… She doesn't need to make a sound."

"Yes, but you do apparently, you silly bitch! Whatever. Fuck you then," Andre huffed, and Elaine laughed, again, despite every effort, and yet over-loudly, as if the greater effort were in sounding sincere. Then…

"She plays the captive," she said softly and to herself, watching her painted lips form the words in the mirror before she looked down at her feet and began to cry. "But Andre, I am truly a captive. I have never been so, so in love…that I ache so in your absence. And I find in your presence that I have lost my capacity to speak, to want my own wants articulately, and so I force myself to say things, noisy, unimportant things just to spite you. But really I am mortified to find myself relegated to only the most inarticulate expressions of my consuming contentment at your hands. I fear utterly irrational fears, like the loss of you. I am humiliated. I am not free. And I am confused and I am angry at how often now I find that I do not remotely wish to *be* free."

And Elaine wept to the empty room, and glanced into the mirror to find him, embarrassed by his witness, and then to the floor again, she wept, until Andre said, his sound coming over her again like an embrace, "My precious darling, this is the truest thing. The bird is not a woman and can never feel love for her captor. If she could she might never leave his glove. And you, divine creature, are not a bird. You can't fly. If you could you might find so much more to love throughout the wide and glorious world than the likes of me, and my note-less mediocrity, that I could never hope to keep you. And I do so want to keep you. It is the falconer's story; he who God grants nothing so sublime as the magic of a woman's spirit, nor the falcon's facility to mount the air and soar. He is no closer to one than the other, and all he can hope for from either, in his wretchedness, is some semblance of inclusion; some symbol of his significance; some sense of control." Elaine looked in the mirror, surveyed the room again, and began to save her eyes from the mess her tears had begun to make of them. "Such eyes should never need to cry," said the steady, honeyed voice, and it made her still when she let it. "To whom do you owe such tears? Each day, my angel, with the set and focus of those eyes that test and observe me, and search me for my utmost, you give me to know in no uncertain terms that I can never tame you. And *I* am the captive. I am slave to the illusion of the power to keep you by my side. And if you allow me to live here in the comfort of that lie, you will never lose me… Now get dressed or you'll be late," Andre barked. "And you know how I hate it when you're late…. Radio telemetry… I oughta slap you…"

"Hmm, perhaps," Elaine conceded as she finished the touches on her make-up and rose unhurriedly from in front of the mirror. "How quickly, Andreas, we both seem to recover from our flights of humility." She said it as if to herself, knowing his inclination to storm from rooms as punctuation to his final remarks. The clock on the dressing table read five fifty-three. She would not be late. She was never late.

She spun about slowly, her eyes sweeping the furniture in a search for something, perhaps to be certain he had gone, but looking across the bed, the dresser top, and on the nightstand as well. Turning back into the mirror, she quickly contemplated her naked throat. The pearl earrings had not been asked for either. She snatched them from her ears and tossed them onto the dressing table like dice. At the bedside she shimmied into her dress, tossed the stockings on the dresser where the thong panties still lay un-thought of, sat to put on her shoes, and her attention was drawn just to her left where there, draped innocently enough upon the bedpost, a lush, deep purple pashmina vibrated its sumptuous super-saturated relevance at her like temptation itself. Within a storm of three seconds, wound in the rush of motion to be on time, she reached for it, checked her reach, then reached again, rising and plucking it up as she walked from the room, sweeping it about her shoulders mumbling to herself, "GPS, women's rights... Who has time to sit around and dream up this bullshit?... Don't these people have lives?... Anyway, it's chilly outside."

The big oaken front door closed behind her with a hearty thud. Elaine, in stunning black, strode, nearly glided down the long, slated walk toward the front gate pulling on her long black satin gloves. Andre would notice immediately, the unsanctioned black, and the just as unasked-for shock of purple swathing her supposed-to-be naked shoulders and back, and he would begin his dance of indignation. And she would go girlish and grin, and wash in the joy of his having come. But even as she would fall about him, and wrap her arms around his head, kissing his eyelids, burying her nose in the warmth of his neck up under his chin, greedily devouring the scent and sense of him, she would not apologize, nor make excuse. Let him level whatever reckoning he might. There would be time enough then to behave.

The early autumn night was still, and as her heels clicked a constant rhythm on the slated walk, two tiny purple porcelain bells jingled in time.

The Odd Purgatory of
My Personal Perception

I can rail at the compulsions of nature or the motion of time, as I tend to most naturally, and ultimately drop dead on time's schedule without a single change in the plan occurring on account of my say-so. The facts do not induce any merciful sense of surrender in me as I might hope they would; a peace in whatever will be inasmuch as I am powerless to affect it. I sometimes undertake to determine what little influence I might have on the course of events and apply it to my self-perceived utmost. But that is simply another long, ambling philosophical road that is probably endless, and leads to the same limbo, where I labor on like a logic-laden Sisyphus pushing up the boulder of being human. It is my road, my limbo. Others have theirs; each a separate set of obsessions striven at, until death, helplessly.

When I met Susan, her name hinted loudly to me at a sort of pedestrian that I think perhaps little girls christened thus will have a tough task in life to rise above whether they ever actually realize the efforts they exert to do so or not. How much thought in the giving could a name so common require? We were both youngish, aspiring actors on Manhattan. We had neither of us been free of the strictures of acting school long enough to be either great at it, or irreparably embittered by its disappointments; about five years… She was gentle as it seemed to me, and light of heart; opened to the world in the ways that an actor must be, but for whom you worry, knowing that the industry, and Manhattan as well, are cruel and can kill without compunction those who are truly emotionally available to their lovelessness. In truth, she was not so much. Almost none are. She was thought-bound like the rest of us, and she strained at the bonds in various directions, some of which were unique, surprising even, and attracting of my attention. And our perspective is relative given how fear infuses our own human reality...but a sweet, clever girl with an immanent care, she seemed to me touchable in some significant way. It was significant, to me, that she was simply, uniquely, more touchable than most. No more than that.

We were both working, separately at first, with a private acting coach; both hoping to better whatever skills we might have had, and better our chances at the lottery of professional success. As we moved from working on monologues, to wanting the more lifelike form of two-person scene work, it was suggested by our coach that we meet with her together, thus changing our two separate sessions and their two separate fees to a single combined session for the same fee split between us that we could then do twice as often. (I should say that a less scrupulous figure in the dubious world of American actor training, which means only a more fear-influenced one, of which variety there are far greater number, would have charged us both the same, as if we were still single clients, never venturing the possibility of us working twice a week for the same dime. But she, it was our fortune, had transcended that at least, even as she negotiated whatever the daily limbo of her own.)

Susan was skinny-fashion-model long, pale, and loose curly blonde. She had those odd proportions that are more art-like than human, and features that, while an acquired taste, tended toward the age-old American standards of feminine beauty but never quite met them, which is to say white girl pretty but not white girl typically pretty, which is to say that, with her decent set of acting skills, she could have been anybody's Nicole Kidman, Gwyneth Paltrow, or Daryl Hannah, Daryl being, at least to me, the least white girl typically pretty of these. Of course, she hadn't an Australian stamp of person to give her market value, or a strategic and publicly aggrandized celebrity marriage to assist her. Nor had she the nepotistic boost of a celebrity parent, all such things so necessary in skewing the odds in one's favor when seeking distinction as an actor in the American industry. So perhaps she could only really have been anybody's Daryl Hannah, all loping length, unruly yellow tresses, and little breasts on the cover, with a more unnamable beauty out from behind gray eyes, not blue as Daryl's were. Some of the names I might try and give to that which she emanated would be "grace," "kindness…" "ingenuousness," I suppose. But descriptors do not express us any better than they define the forces that we let drive us through lives unto death. To name them anything is as impotent an act as to live on in their governance without question. That said, better, I guess, to be governed by "grace," even if it's just a word, than by "fear."

Susan had a boyfriend or something. I only saw him once when he picked her up in his work truck, after our coaching session, from the street corner I'd walked her to at the appointed time to wait. He looked, from the cab of his truck, like the run-of-the-mill, blue-collar white boy that she had at some point described to me. Lean-faced… Much of her description and what I recall about seeing him myself has faded into generalities. In fact, much of what has ever been told me about others' romantic relationships—as I recall it all, almost unfailingly, as an ever-shifting combination of contrived connections, compromises, and quasi-estrangements—has blended together to compose the generic image my mind calls forth of what becomes of our aspirations to love. I'm sure he was somehow handsome. I assumed that he could be tender, or seductive, or funny; that she was moved by his bravado, or his boyishness, or perhaps how, in the darkness, he confided to her his fears.

Perhaps the air of a working man that he moved in, its smells, conjuring the sense in her that he could provide, that she would be protected; perhaps some of these, all these, any of these, stirred up in an intricate philter allayed with some parts simplicity, and a haircut aroused her. Who knows... They were together in some form that, despite any hackneyed analysis of mine, was a thing that I was bound to respect. And soon after, she was pregnant.

We continued to meet and work with our acting coach for six months as her pregnancy progressed. We even searched for and found pregnant characters for her to play in the scene study material we chose. I wondered when, with all that was ever more obviously arriving, she thought she'd be free to ply the skills that she was continuing to sharpen in our work. I wondered when she supposed there would be time to be an actor. But I never asked.

To me, in the odd purgatory of my personal perception, pregnancy has always been a look much more aesthetically borne by barnyard animals. Borne by Susan, who was tall and thin, the abdominal malformation caused by the gestating fetus rather resembled the distended bellies we too often see of starving African children. I have seen dogs, and cats, and horses, and cows, and pigs grow apparently more fat in the bearing of their offspring, but they have always only looked to me like fatter cows, pigs, and horses. Only in women have I ever seen the extreme, and to me, grotesque changes of form that accompany the bringing forth of new life. And I have found it unfair and unkind. I feel robbed of women, even those with whom I haven't the remotest connection, particularly when the process is set on thoughtlessly, as if by instinct, like insects do. The part of every woman that I own outright; my perception of her perfection, in this collision of bestial inclination and personal prerogative, is inevitably burgled from in front of my very eyes. The wonder-inspiring intensity of the feminine, sharpened by intellect, is then rudely, clumsily adulterated by some energy apparently more of the bovine in nature, and my reverence is in equal measure attrited. This is very hard. Many will argue, "Not as hard as having a baby." But I didn't choose hardship… And of course this perspective of mine could never be met with much other than indignation by those to whom I might express it. But I think, surely, that is because the indignant have been taught to be so; taught that, because it is inevitable, you must find reasons to call it lovely, or even sublime, and that you are obliged to effuse acrimony at the indecorous suggestion that it is only, in fact, animal and uninspired; strictly down on the farm.

I knew that Susan would never go back to the way she was, neither in life nor form. I knew that her thin, fair skin would never again look as though it had been tailored by God to fit her frame once it had been stretched in every direction by child in utero, and gnawed upon by child at breast. Do cows ever require episiotomies? And while she seemed from the first resolved to carrying this baby to term, she did not ever seem to me to wax particularly enthusiastic about it, nor to speak of the father in any terms that suggested anything more than a promised uncertainty. There was an inexorability about her pregnancy; a lusterless acceptance of circumstance and forward motion that I have forever watched, and that I yearned this time for nothing so much as to halt with a fist in its face; a deferring to the forms that she infused with the idea of beauty when it seemed she could muster it. And indeed she did, simply by being beautiful herself, gracious, and gentle. The complex and comely can get away with that more readily, certainly, than the simple and homely can. But at the end of the day, there is still boy, girl, a bit of chemically doctored miscommunication, baby, life… What but this? And I thought, what of art? Not that which you make, but that which you are… What of you? I thought this, but never said it. How *do* you say it? How do you say, "Come, let us die now. This moment. In beauty and arrogance, acquiescing to nothing. Because what comes commonly is no respecter of our uniqueness. It will not be pretty, what comes. We will never be more unlike everyone than we are right now. So let us come together and love, earnestly impassioned and reckless without the need to make it mean; to make it signify or presage; without the need to leave anything of ourselves here behind other than the echoes of our gorgeous, incendiary congress built upon nothing but beauty and this moment. Then die, and be gone from fear, and instinct, and the commonality of beasts; from purgatory."

There were years then following that I lost sight of Susan. I went on to pursue career goals, happy that there were other beautiful things for me to look at and stand near along the often so ugly way. News eventually trickled in from somewhere deep in New Jersey that the man had gone, that Susan sold real estate, that her mother was there somewhere, and that the little girl was thriving. Through our mutual acquaintances I was even to learn that Susan traveled into Manhattan from time to time to pursue an acting audition or two. This I was heartened to hear and admired, though it seemed to make a hobby out of the work she had once striven so fervently to make bear fruit. She had been great with *that* child first; great with a thing conceived and gestating just as assuredly within her, being brought forth in labor, fed and nurtured with love. Why had *that* pregnancy been terminated? Was it only for the sake of this other one, less abstract, and more easily labeled "a good thing, a beautiful thing, a sacred thing to do and to be?" Why didn't you believe that you were good enough, sacred enough? An abortion is an abortion, unnatural and invasive and intent on destruction. It tears at the innards and something is left behind, a vivisection of the spirit that is forever injured and unable to heal. A creative abortion, the abortion of a divine idea is no less tragic, no less mournful than that of a fetus, and leaves no less inevitably a scar. The fetus was not there. It was later, much later that you coupled with some boy and succumbed to biology. Had not the urgings of God been romancing you long before that, inseminating your dreams, and filling you with sacred expression? Weren't *you* the child? And where did you go? Why were you not born?

On one of her trips into the city, having at last spoken, we managed to meet. It was in front of the mall that was once The New York Coliseum to the west of Columbus Circle. It was wintertime on Manhattan, quite cold, and Susan had said I would recognize her by the bright pink parka she'd be wearing. I laughed, assuming I'd need no such markers. But I did indeed see it first; one of those puffy, down-filled things made of nylon or some other plastic utility cloth that the stately, urban, un-owned Susan of six years before would not have been caught dead in. The color alone suggested a lack of aesthetic sense, or what I, having known her, could only imagine was a dismissal of that sense for the sake of matters arisen that were far more significant and pressing. Either way, it shouted at me of the everyday, the workaday, the commonplace that I had always thought one should do anything to keep one's life from becoming. It was a mother and baby color, a New Jersey suburban color, a Middle-American color, a thoughtless color.

And we sat.

And smiled a lot.

She seemed small inside the big pink parka. Her skin was dry and drawn. Her lips were chapped. Her hands were tiny, fragile, and blue. Her hair was short. And she looked, above all, used by all things except herself. Somewhere in the course of our conversation she offered, casually, "My body is a mess," even though I had not asked. It arose, as simply and unguarded as the rejoinder to "What do you take in your coffee?" And I felt ashamed that she knew what I was sitting there thinking, and that she felt somehow answerable. I felt small, and wondered if I looked so to her. And I said, "I'm sure it's not," instead of "Why?" And I said, "You look well," instead of "What the fuck?!"

And we sat.

And drank coffee.

And she told me of her life in brief.

And they say such strange things as, "She's amazing. She's so beautiful. She's the best thing that I've ever done with my life." And I suspect, as I listen, that it would not be politic, nor at all productive for them to say instead, "It was all a mistake. My biology and psychology conspired to betray me, and now they are both entirely in the service of other people and things. I don't know why I did this." As I listened I was aware that I could never fathom motherhood until I had ovaries, and that, as me; as a thing so drastically removed from womanhood, I really had no right to try. She might not have been suppressing any such thoughts. Who am I to know? She might have been wholly sincere. Wholly happy. Feeling wholly relevant. It was only how wholly otherwise she looked, as appearing to my self-ish, self-serving sight; if not guilty of a ponderous error, then stalwartly resolved—to the detriment and denial of all that was of her alluring and youthful and intensely free and wondrous to me—resolved to a life promising hardship, one supremely disinterested in her divinity, wandered into without a fight… Or hardly a thought… Even chosen. Imagine that!

When we parted company after leaving Martha Rogers' studio that last time and walking through the frozen rain to the subway, there was nothing to scream. She was six months along, an infinitely far easier thing to be *after* you become anybody's Daryl Hannah, even without a constant partner, and even with all the dysfunction that your fragile mind can amass still tearing at the fabric of your life. But there was nothing to be said about it now.

What I remember distinctly about Susan is her laugh, and her bearing, and her height. I remember her acting, how good it was already, in the studio, and there perhaps as well at the top of the subway steps…better than mine. And I remember how she used to say she liked the trace of bourbon on my breath after cocktails we'd have when our sessions were over (cocktails *I'd* have ultimately, because she was pregnant). I remember how she made a case about that then, how she held the space to make it in, forcefully claiming that trivial awareness because it moved her in the moment, and how that was enough to take ownership, and shamelessly to let her face and posture express it, that she liked it and was peeved because she could not have her own… Her own what? Bourbon? Me? Her own way?

And I remember lingering on the street above the subway station wanting an answer why they trade the things that make them most beautiful, most unique; why they trade the original idea that God had in them for the one thing that any dumb bitch, any barnyard animal with a working womb can be and do.

You can talk to me of the biological clock, of the primal drives toward child bearing, and I have nothing with which to dispute you other than to point at the multitude of God's creatures whose lives and deaths are no more than random because their brains are not big enough for them to aspire to anything beyond it. They cannot choose but procreate…and eat, and defecate, and die. And there is something beatific in that, I imagine, if one is a camel or a codfish. What higher beauty for them? What need for feats of genius that awe the world, and that they alone are capable of? What need for anything but perhaps the most thoughtless drivers of life?

The other memories are indistinct. They blend and soften because they are of things so common. We can plunge our strong, vigorous hands that God gave us to grasp at our dreams deep into the well of cumulative rationale and come up with any old pedestrian fists full of distracting choices and reasons, and run with them, never thinking of how, if we hold them too tightly too long, they will turn our hands tiny, and fragile, and blue.

That night above the 1 train, I knew I would never see Susan, *that* Susan, again, and I said goodbye, wanting the release of hollering futile things instead, like "Don't!" and "Stop!" and "Wake the fuck up!" Instead I chose civility from the well of rationale, and I walked down Broadway in the icy wet knowing neither of us would have what we wanted because we went along, inexorably. I held civility tightly in my cold, clenched fists, which seemed smaller, and not so strong as they had. And I wondered when life would begin.

Liza and  Isaac

The involuntary spasms of joy that would overcome him, infrequently, but utterly, manifesting in an uncharacteristic silliness that rendered him nearly unrecognizable, even to himself, were to him a frustration. He felt himself afflicted by such playful intrusions, for these sudden transformations toward the light were not whole, but rather ejaculations of mirth spotted with self-consciousness, and qualified by doubt. And they tended to rob credibility, despite his best efforts, from melancholy, his most natural default among the ways of being; his miserable bastardship… It was a credibility that was self-bestowed, and so he alone tended to experience the loss. Others, meeting him for the first time on the occasion of just such an episode, knew only what they saw, and tended rather to feel bereft once the fit had had its course and passed, never having known that it had been a temporary condition.

The 2 A.M. waitress with the 4 A.M. eyes minding the coffee counter of the diner was nearly delirious with the lack of something that might have been sleep. She dragged a rag across the clean, unused counter top, fiddled with dispensers of salt, sugar, napkins, and straws, emptied old coffee and brewed more afresh, and was either venting a restless energy or trying to summon any at all by absently drumming with two spoons upon the register when he walked in. She was relieved to see him. She would have been pleased to see anyone who wasn't the cook or the manager, but he was reserved, and serious, and sad, and such made him peculiarly relevant to her, and handsome, so much so that she stopped her futzing and stood, stark still, waiting with an interest in where he would choose to sit. He'd looked about, his hands in his coat pockets, and eyed a far corner booth as he'd advanced into the place, slowed slightly, but all the while walking forward toward where she stood. And he took to a stool at the end of the empty row nearest to her and the register, looked at her softly and smiled. She saw his smile as if struggling up through a low-grade, un-assaultive disquiet that defined his demeanor entire. It defined not just his mood, but his beauty; a dignified troubled that became him, like his long double-breasted gray wool coat, allover thread bare and tattered at the sleeves ends, but fitting and somehow refined regardless. And it was thus defined that he sat through three cups of coffee spent staring mostly into the cup, saying nothing but, "Thank you" each time she returned with the pot. She concocted reasons to go elsewhere in the place so that she wouldn't be perceived to be standing there staring at him, as she was, and would have preferred to have been left alone to do. And he glanced up only briefly upon each return, desultorily, perhaps simply to make sure she'd received his gratitude.

And so... It came as a surprise to them both to discover that his spirit had, sometime in the thirty minutes passed, surreptitiously slipped the bonds of melancholia where he kept it, and suddenly came bursting through the veil of concern he wore, through his sadness and weight, and all that made him handsome; came bursting through with big eyes and noise like a circus clown into a funeral, and she was spellbound, smiling broadly to see him jump in shock when she handed him the check upon which she had scribbled the figure of a dollar and eighty seven cents that his counter tab had come to.

"Puppies and kittens and little woodland creatures!" he boomed aloud, bobbling the check at his finger's ends with the plosive P of "puppies" giving a jolt to the shoulders and arms and a staccato shuffle to the feet, followed by a pronouncedly self-conscious looking about the abandoned eatery to see whom he might have disturbed, or who else was witness to his exaggerated dilemma. Then he threw back his coat, and hiked up a pair of old but elegant and yet appropriately clown-like high-waisted pants, and with an absurd ostentation, conjuring from her a giggle, he pulled from his fat pocket all of some twelve or thirteen odd bucks, licked his thumb, said, "Let's see here…" and started to count, like he was counting into a roll of two or three grand. He lost his count twice, would wave the few bills around in a grandiose flourish of arms, wipe his nose, lick his thumb, furrow his brow in concentration and start again. When he stopped in his counting a third time to take a thoughtful breath, again look furtively about the room and then at her, his face in absolute earnest, and asked her if she had two tens for a five, she, entranced by his instant vaudeville, opened the register and had nearly handed him the bills before she'd realized. Then they both laughed, and he told her she laughed like an angel, though all in the course of saying as much he was distracted by the thought that it was a ridiculous thing to say. Not purposefully ridiculous, as he was once accident had given birth to the jester in him, but pathetically ridiculous, as in without even the pretense of his own authority—altogether cliché—laughing like an angel—What do angels laugh like? Rallying focus to arrive at "No matter," or some cerebral derivation thereof, he slapped himself in the head a couple of times attempting to make it quiet down. She watched him do it and laughed some more, thinking it must be a part of the act. She didn't seem to disapprove the compliment, and asked him instead, as she let loose the bun of her thick, brown hair only to pull it back from her face again and secure it in a ponytail, where he was going next.

"Probably home to bed," he said, "seein' as to how it's so late it's early, but in point of factuality, I have been prostitutin' over that very question for the past many minutes and was wonderin' if you had any...um...whatcha call...um... suggestions." Sometimes a well-placed malaprop, or any odd other grammatical abuse, spoken with conviction to a sympathetic audience is sexier than anything else the night can offer up. It's never simply the words themselves. Of course it's not. It's the hour, and the desire to escape the weight of everything that isn't funny pressing in upon the heart of the one who speaks them, and of the one to whom they're spoken. It's the eyes that watch the mouth that makes them. And a fleeting moment of absolute trust in good and perfection that the exchange occurs within. Liza giggled, blushed, and, finding courage unrestrainedly, nearly involuntarily, going forth before her like he found the ghosts of Leo Gorcey, proposed a better plan.

But by morning, whimsy had vanished. It had fled in the night while he slept, his rascal familiar not ever to be trusted, and Isaac woke to the more comforting exertions of wrestling with the legions of his own useless thoughts. In his accustomed mind into his unaccustomed surroundings he rose, pulled on his pants, and sat stilly on the edge of his last night's lover's bed, who had awakened to his rustlings, and now sat watching him with a questioning expression that bespoke confusion; a wondering as to where he whom she had come to know so sweetly in the night had gone, flavored by the feeling perhaps that, having known him so briefly (only for hours really), she had no right to ask. She didn't ask. And Isaac volunteered nothing by way of explanation. He had none. But he held her face, and then he kissed her, a kiss that was not big but lasting—the kind in which sometimes at least good intention can be communicated free of any other agenda—before pulling away and pulling on his coat and leaving in a silence of apology.

In the courtyard of the building several large fish glided about in a small, well-attended pond. Isaac approached thinking still. Thinking how was it possible that a graveyard shift waitress in a diner could afford even a modest apartment in a building with a fish pond that was actually kept, and in which the fish looked happy? And what do happy-looking fish look like…? Isaac smacked himself upside the head again two or three times as the "happy-looking" fish came to the edge and close to the surface to contemplate his frenetic motions. They bobbed about observing Isaac as she had just shortly before, mouths a little agape, eyes wide and unblinking. And he stared back, planted there with his long coat open and thrust behind, and his hands dug deep into voluminous pants pockets of warm, winter tweed, while the chill fall wind stirred the leaves in circles around the courtyard and his feet, until the communion was broken by a voice from over his shoulder saying, "They're carp," and Isaac turned to see Liza barefoot in a bathrobe, hair falling loose about her face. "Ya know, goldfish," she said, her sound deeper and more resonant with the morning than he'd remembered from the night before. "These are just big ones. People like to call them koi because it sounds pretty, and they *are* pretty. But they're really just big, stupid, inedible fish. Well…you *could* eat them… People do. Anyway, they're perpetually hungry and that thing they're doing is a trained response to being fed. That's the only reason they're interested in you at all. They think you're going to feed them." Isaac turned back to the marine life and considered that, while Liza hugged her robe about her and watched.

"And if you had to choose one," he said, "would you rather go through life being called 'carp' or 'koi?'"

"Just what the fuck is your problem?!" Liza's strident retort, blasting forth before the last of his question had quite left his mouth, her voice, risen again in pitch, ricocheted about the courtyard startling pigeons and Isaac alike as he turned to her again sharply. "It's cold out here," she said in a less accusatory tone returned to a lower register, but looking as if she'd even startled herself a little.

"Yeah," said Isaac. "You see, I know that." And they looked at one another until Isaac looked at the ground, as if to find the next thing to say that might be hidden there just beneath the swirling leaves. "You got…I don't know…ya got oatmeal or somethin' in there?"

"Yeah," she said, as though the answer should have been obvious, and waited. "Well…okay…" he said. "I really didn't want you to go off thinkin' you was just two hips that passed through my sight… Two hips…" he said again having gauged no change in her expression, but only her still studying of him. "Two hips that pass…"

"That's funny, Isaac," she said before he could further explain. "*You're* funny," she said without a smile.

"Yeah," he said. And you're kind, he thought.

As they walked back towards the building together, even as

he slipped his hand into hers and squeezed it only tightly enough for it to mean anything, Isaac was already thinking how maybe he was only there because he wanted to be fed.

Liza was thinking she'd rather be called "koi."

Roxanne,
Larry,
and
Lynn

The waitress at the café wore pink.

On Sundays, it was a breakfast place where the chronically penurious indigenous creatures, awaking slowly from their Saturday nights, could still eat affordable omelets, and sip cocktails into the afternoon. It was an odd cart of amenity that had preceded the horse of gentrification not yet crept into that part of Brooklyn. A ragtag, tumbledown storefront of eclectic wall hangings, candle-lit of evenings, and buoyant with ambient music, the looping playlists of young artists interested in the quality of sounds more than the content of songs. And there was a year, as short as a year is (still longer for them than for their elders, and before they were all as faded footnotes in the gentrifying conquest of the boroughs); a year that its owners, having pieced it together out of nothing for creativity's sake, were unaware that the price they could ask for the artistic innovations of their indigence was about to rise exponentially. That year, the new bohemians, destitute as they were, presided, while the older natives of that neighborhood stuck to coffee and egg-on-a-roll in the diner on the next block. Those were the old-schoolers, the disco fabulous, the hope of the eighties and nineties since grown into the unremarkable and irrelevant, whose days were a struggle, whose sleeps were disturbed by dreams of doom in the time coming on. Even their hopes for their children were frayed, and seemed to them no longer reasonable, so that they did not speak of them.

But some of the children were these, the painters and guitar players, spoken word poets and the sundry creatively aspiring, estranged from their progenitors, living on shit-a-week, who had known nothing in their thirty years or less on Earth but broken government, and the flourishing nihilism that the avaricious elite had cultivated and left the natives of Brooklyn and everywhere to stew and die in. And now the wealthy were returning. Of these distant shapers of places and policies the hipsters were aware only in the abstract. For that brief year, they could be. The world was larger than theirs, the only "un-acquired" corner of Williamsburg, but all that they knew as relevant to them was there. And it was relevant to others, their vivid, uncensored youth and its ever-evolving expression. And soon the moneyed would return to wear their clothes, and affect their postures, to renovate the leaky lofts where they now squatted, fucked, and dreamed, to pay thrice the price for the three eggs that made an omelet, and to live pretending that they were them, but rich and owning things.

For now, for them, to do two weeks' worth of laundry, or to indulge in two hours of this nourishing Sunday ritual, celebrating the survival of another week, was never a contest. They began to stir by noon, woke, smoked, reached for one another across sheets scented with body oils, semen, and sweat, slept again, but seemed always to find themselves at the café by one. Their garments were wear-worn and piebald, and looked always slightly soiled fresh from the dryer anyway, patched together like their laptops and their instruments, and their art, and their day-to-day lives, and like them. They were cobbled together as a culture as well by the social catalysts of new chemical compounds ingested at parties, and by the commonality of an as yet unsmitten sense of trust in beauty over practicality, fueled by the indomitability of youth's audacious dreams, and the social media.

And the waitresses wore pink…

It was that perfectly ugly or pretty pink, depending perhaps on mood, residual alcohol, or caffeine correction. She wore a pink sweat suit that accentuated her olive skin and made her dark eyes the unavoidable focus of her face. She wrapped her head in a matching pink scarf tied in a knot behind and trailed down her back amidst a cascade of curly black hair like a pirate. A large silver hoop swinging from each earlobe lent only a further authenticity to that whole buccaneer sensibility she had operating from the shoulders up. But it was only a thing. Like a model in an erotic Halloween clothing catalogue doing the sexy swashbuckler. She was far too perfectly pretty to be a real pirate. And far too petite. And then, there were the rounded toes of her white sneakers peeking out from beneath the draping hems of her pink sweat pants.

She introduced herself as Roxanne, and Larry repeated languidly but smiling, "Roxanne." Larry in repose, the king of his own corner of the café where, at this hour, just enough sunlight drifted in across him and Lynn, first through the leaves in the tree outside, then through the blinds, to paint them dappled and lovelier still, as handsome a couple as they were, though any more would have been buzz-kill enough to make them move to another booth. Larry, or "Brother Love," or "My Man," or "*Papi*," when Lynn spoke to him, a different name for each different way that the light framed his face from moment to moment through those golden hours that seemed only to take on that particular quality on Sundays.

"Roxanne," he said again. "…She's the buccaneer vixen of the seven seas and Flatbush…" And the rest of the rhyming couplet that then went on to compose itself in his head concluded with "Brazilian or a fat bush." But because he was only just slightly more decorous than to recite it, he had at least to laugh. His indolent chortle Roxanne flashed her brilliant teeth and giggled back at, probably because she presumed her tip depended upon it. Lynn, reclining against Larry, her arm twined about his, and at their length their fingers interlaced and enwrapping the same huge, potter's creation of a coffee mug, Lynn, perusing her hungrily through the early Sunday A.M. tangles of thick black mane that draped her face, wasn't sure that the child had understood the pirate reference at all.

Roxanne tried to rattle off the brunch specials, but Larry refused to let her. "I don't know if you look more like a pirate, or a packet of Sweet-n-Low," he said, hardly animated still, his warm, sleepy eyes, heavy-lidded, wandering the length of her standing there shifting from foot to foot like a bashful twelve-year-old.

A man can say something that will shatter any illusions a woman holds of him in an instant. Lynn sucked her teeth and said, "Stupid! You just called huh saccharine, *pendejo!*"

Their hands still held the cup. She leaned into him still, but her admonition, spoken in that tonality of impending fury that Latin chicks had, slicing through the soundscape and making people look, it made Larry wince a little and stiffen, sitting up slightly in his corner to defend, "I called her sweet—"

But Lynn leaning all the harder, her soft, sex-scented density pressing him into his seat and preventing him from assuming his fighting posture, insisted, "Nah, nah, nah, *escúcheme*. You called huh a sugah substitute. You shouldn't evah speak until after three o'clock on Sundays. Fuckin' *cállate*."

The Latina of the boroughs, the Puerto Rican variety particularly, has a peculiar skill. A spectacular and frightening thing to see, she can downshift from rage through general annoyance into slow, smoldering, unabashed lust in three seconds, or in the time it takes to exhale, or to execute a languorous shift of focus that ends when her dark, consuming eyes come to rest on things more appetizing.

To Roxanne, looking to Lynn ever more delectably bewildered, she said, "I apologize fuh him, my Love," as she slowly raked her great, unwashed tresses back from her face with her free hand, revealing to the waitress the dubious intent in the patient ferocity of her stare. "*Diga*...um, say da specials..." she about moaned.

With Larry sufficiently chastened, and Lynn all eyes, Roxanne was able to get through the list and into a thick, uncomfortable silence that the admiring lovers presided over with obvious amusement; like a couple of cartoon vultures contemplating a cute, fat mouse.

"Coffee is good right now, Baby," Lynn said, ending the deliberation, but not her unmerciful ogling of the waitress as if she were the most prominent of confections upon a tray of deserts. "But come back in a very little, ya know, few minutes, would you, and we'll figyah somethin' else out." She smiled as if she might bite next—reaching out with her free hand for just one gentle stroke of the hand that was reaching for the menus—a big, freshly fucked, early morning, greedy, Sunday grin. Roxanne, flustered and fidgeting in some embarrassing space of unexpected arousal in between frustrated and flattered, smiled too as her face flushed, and hurried off, stumbling a little over the hems of her sweatpants as she went.

Larry had to lean forward in his seat, wriggling with effort just a bit out from under Lynn's full body press, to watch the pink sway of Roxanne from under his leaden lids as she walked toward the kitchen.

"Whadya reckon," he drawled. "She's gotta be what, a buck 0 five soakin' wet?"

He fell back in the booth and brought the coffee mug to his face bringing Lynn's hand with it. He kissed it, one knuckle to the next, and between jewelry and intricately painted nails, and she rolled her head slowly back from where Roxanne had disappeared through the swinging kitchen door to ponder him, the second such Brooklyn Latina languorous shift of focus that day...

" 'Soakin' wet,' hunh?" she intoned through her lascivious grin as she watched Larry nibbling the back of her middle finger. "How's it taste, *Papi*?"

"It would taste better with a little Sweet-n-Low on it," he said, and then began to giggle, the light through the blinds shifting about on his laughing face, the darkening shadow of a beard unable to disguise the incorrigible child.

God's Children

She was God's child, so he had thought; one of the ones that the Universe looks after because, for whatever reason, they didn't end up here upon this seething orb of self-serving fuck-ups with the tools to fend for themselves, so he thought... Dumber than a box of rocks, he'd thought, but as delicate and as lovely as an orchid. And she smelled like vanilla ice cream. She was the sort of vacuous that could be beyond sexy when the sexy wore it. And he had not been looking for a lover that would be anything more than that: sexy, immediate, and unencumbering ever after. He had few other reasons to subject himself to a barroom's sensory barrage of boisterous humanity. Everywhere else, feeling the oppressive weight of its incurious tumbling on, he navigated around the dumb motion of the masses as best his own too human condition could manage. The only thing to be gotten by braving the concentration of festering crowd psychology that a Friday night tavern contained was the prize of some pretty diversion intent on receiving him without superfluous ceremony; something sweet and soft to distract his embattled heart and sate his hunger for an hour or two without making of itself a nuisance in the A.M., and she came dancing up to him from out of the aggregate of noise and dark and compressed bodies in a joint in Seattle, and stood at the bar staring at him, blankly, as her hips swayed to the bass beat of The Isley Brothers singing "Caravan of Love." She was waif-like and boyish, and yet a salient feminine insistence perfused the air around her. It imbued her formlessness, and seduced by waiting, patiently, present more than purposeful, vacantly expectant, available more than inviting, to be seduced. And when she turned from him and leaned across the bar to ask the bartender for tequila, he found himself staring at a tattoo of Winnie the Pooh holding a red balloon floating upward between her shoulder blades. He said it "bespoke" her when she returned to him. And when she stared back at the comment with the same serene, unresponsive expression superimposed upon her gentle face, neither acceptance nor rejection in her eyes of green, he assumed that she didn't know the word, "bespeak," or what it would have had to do with her tattoo.

She handed him a double shot, and threw another down her throat. And then she stood stone still and watched him, waiting for him to follow, and waiting attentively on the liquor to find some place in her belly that stirred something beyond impassivity. When it did, she smiled—a thick, kissing mouth—almost too broadly for her fine features. Then waited again. Then he drank. And she began again to sway, her narrow hips holding afloat, by some anomaly of physics, or feat of sublime witchcraft, a pair of beltless cargo pants, as if they hung precariously by invisible hooks upon her pelvic bones, and might, upon nothing more than the right thought rising to qualify the air between them, fall from her waist and surrender to him her sex beneath.

She drank too much when she went clubbing, and knew it was a problem, with reasons that, like so many things, she couldn't with any ease articulate. She was inarticulate, wordless mostly, which only lent credibility to the perception, his perception, she knew, that she was, indeed, God's child. And why not, she owned unarticulated. Life is simpler when people don't want much of you because they assume that there's so little from you that they can expect. And if you're a pretty woman on top of that, and the thing that they most often want is really the only thing that you ever really want from them... You could do worse than to be thought witless. So, while she had perceptions and pronouncements of her own regarding the perceptions and pronouncements of others with regard to her, she was aware of none worth voicing or arguing over, particularly at the hour; particularly as the raggedy, speed rail tequila was tardily beginning to do what it had been paid to; particularly when, as with him, so much of the world around her made her hurt, and fucking felt so good, then eating, then laughing, then dancing. The eating and the laughing could take turns for second place. But, if she could have the first of those, she could generally keep her judgments to herself.

And in the morning, one such tacit discernment was that he, with his broad, laborer's shoulders, dolce down-south speech, and panty-remover brown eyes, was a surprisingly non-repugnant manifestation materializing on the daylight side of an over-indulgent evening out. Attraction after the fact was rare in her world; downright surprising to find herself *re*-aroused by the smell of his skin stirred with the smell of vanilla she'd left there. And so it was icing—vanilla icing—on an already tasty cake to discover that he even had a job. It wasn't just any job either, but a job that only a kind person would have. And she ached for kindness beneath her un-asking expressions. He read to children at the library and the community center for what couldn't even have put gas in that rattletrap, green Ford pick-up he drove. He liked words. She liked that he liked them. And so she found it no great task to forgive him for saying things like, "it bespeaks you," and arrogantly presuming that she had no idea what he was talking about. And he had an unflagging libido, and an unpredictable sense of humor peeking out shyly from beneath an otherwise solemn demeanor that read as strength to her, all of which she silently searched for but seldom expected to find in a lover unobscured by all of the human nature that rendered so many to her so barely worth the effort to engage.

He also, she discovered, had the Kanji characters for the word loosely translated as "clown" tattooed across the nape of his neck. This, he explained to her, some mean-spirited tattoo artist in Chinatown, New York had told him meant "warrior." He had gotten it when he was sixteen, because, he told her, "I was a dumb-ass tryin' ta ack like a mean-ass once. Still am…still do…sometime…shit…" And so she saw that he *knew* that he was occasionally utterly insufferable, which relieved her of any latent pressure to ever make a point of it. "And as it appears that the nomenclature is ineradicable," he said, "I guess the worst thing ain't makin' a few folks laugh. Ya feel me?" which was precisely the right thing to say to her, though she gave away none of it. But she stayed, and waited, and listened to the airs of intellectual superiority escaping from him sporadically on his speech conspicuously smattered in self-deprecation and East Coast urbanisms while his Georgia drawl dripped from a ten-dollar word in every third or fourth sentence he spoke. But mostly she watched, seeing how he gestured, touched, and held things with his hands that reached for her gently, but could break stuff easily. She watched him haltingly struggle up through anxiety to an ungainly embrace of her unexpected and extended presence, barking his frustration at the parking attendant instead, telling him to "do something valuable with his sorry life," and making her laugh aloud, knowing the poor man was receiving the brunt of the wrath that rightly should have been leveled at her and her uninvited still being there. She watched and saw a reverence in him for the very old and the very young, how it was only in their presence that his power and impetuosity was quelled by his kindness and consideration. She laughed when, in navigating the personas that people made of him, his face would look like that of a confused dog who'd been given two or three conflicting commands at once. He heard her laughing, saw her laughing, and he would not deny that his heart was easier for it.

And she took him for what he explained to her about himself, he always thinking she needed to be explained to, and for the evidence of her eyes and other senses, because he was not ordinary, with few words she took him, a somewhat sad-faced, gentle, easy-to-look-at, arm-strong oxymoron of an intermittently condescending, but unpretentious wandering vagabond bemused by his own inherent honesty, who stretched the truth some when he said he was a cabinetmaker but really just read to children in libraries for beer money. She took him with her hungry mouth searching out her wants with fervent intent upon his body. Without asking she took greedily, in silence, except for here, a rare and whispered reproach rising, "gently," and there, a rarer inducement, "Ah! Suck that, dude!" uttered hoarsely as she rode his face, less insistent than imploring. And he would feel sometimes in his acquiescence more utilitarian than desired. But his concession seemed to bring hints of wicked mirth to her icy green eyes, and to make that huge smile play in the corners of her open mouth as she, sweat soaked with her rhythmic panting breaths, head thrown back and an occasional "Fuck yeah!" took him. And, in among all that, he was, he found, he worried, mostly, peculiarly, unfamiliarly content.

The tattoo artist, in his inexplicably angry attack, had dug deep with his needle, and so the dark green characters adorning the back of his neck were slightly raised upon the flesh so that one could read them like Braille. She always held on fiercely there, as she took him, squeezing the muscle over which the writing was indelibly etched, pulling him to her as if taking dominion over his function, and not letting go until he had fulfilled his purpose to her satisfaction. And afterwards, while he was still inside her, as she would stretch her length like a cat and stir about until she found a position atop him that fit for sleeping, she would stroke the soft fuzz where his hairline faded into skin, petting the gentle scarring there, where the word that meant something like "clown," but was meant to mean "warrior" testified to her as his heart beat its strong, slowing, rhythm upon her breastbone.

And she stayed with him in his tiny ground floor illegal sublet off an alley in Fremont, where they fucked each other senseless, marveling at the lust-driven mechanics of it, and laid about in post-coital trances for most of November through March, dumbfounded by contentment in one another's beauty, listening to the daily visitations of the Seattle rain ring the lids of the dumpsters in the alley until starvation made them stir. And sometimes she'd say things, like "Let's get food," and "Good morning…"

And then, on the first day of spring, she said, just as she'd tossed the last of her bags on a small pile by the door, "I'm out."

Then she stepped into him and, pulling him to her by the waist and by the neck, she said, "It bespeaks you."

He backed away to look at her, but she, pulling him to her again and taking to her tiptoes so as to speak into his ear said, "The big, green tattoo…" as she stroked it. "I feel it. I feel you. I felt you when I saw you."

And he backed away again. She letting him go this time, he knelt down to tie the laces of his sneakers, saying as he did, "That's more sentences than I heard you string together in the past four months."

"I never had much to say to you," she said.

Honesty, like love, no matter how sought as the ostensible source of happy in the happily ever after, is often hardly recognized in its unadulterated state. It can look like insensitivity since it has nothing to prove.

"Yeah?" he said, as he stood back up.

And she stepped back into him and reached behind him and up once more with her arms. Pulling him to her, she sought his lips with her nose, and then with her thick mouth, and he kissed her then—that hungry mouth—kissed it until, impassioned, he drew his hands from his pockets and reached down and through her legs and lifted her up on one arm toward the ceiling. From above, riding a big, capable bicep, his huge hand spread and planted between her shoulder blades—where Winnie the Pooh held on tightly to the string of that big red balloon, rising up and out from beneath the grasp of his fingers, not looking particularly concerned about where it would take him—she'd looked down at him; watched him kissing her about the belly, watched, blankly, the way she looked at things, and at people, and saw them more clearly for being in no hurry. She watched him denying her her feet and the floor, so swift and insistent, mercurial and war-like, and she smiled. She watched the way he held his face to her belly, how he lifted her shirt with his nose like a big obdurate old dog, pressing her hard against him with one solid arm and stayed, kissing her there as if it were the holy altar of God, and wept. She felt him weeping, felt the tremor of emotion in the arm that offered her up exaltedly to the sky. She felt the warm tears drop and run down the skin of her belly and gather, absorbed by the waistband of her jeans. She felt him weeping, and holding her soft, warm, muscled belly pressed against his face.

She stroked his hair, and said again, "I feel you." Then she said again, "I'm out."

Returning

There has been music in these days of mine alone;
     mouths to kiss while laughing,
And those soft, intentioned presses of some pretty girl's hands.

(Though not so much as in some right world's own
     should rush, in his huge solitude,

To fill a not so young man's fantasy's demands.)

There **are** those things that, where I've walked, I've done—
     and places, though I would, I did **not** go—

Where rumors I've, without a doubt, begun,
     while others I have lent perspective, so...

I'll come home now.

I have not slept well all these long nights gone.

And I've aches that beg, sweet Love, you lay your hands upon.

—For DKS, 10/9/98